Berlin Baghdad Bombay

Mahir Salih

Published by Mahir Salih, 2025.

This is a work of fiction. Similarities to real people, places, or events are entirely coincidental.

BERLIN BAGHDAD BOMBAY

First edition. January 16, 2025.

Copyright © 2025 Mahir Salih.

ISBN: 979-8230489511

Written by Mahir Salih.

With thanks to Penny Allsop for editing and Stan for publishing.

Chapter One

Escape from Berlin (1940)

It was a bright, mid-June day in Berlin. The streets lay unusually still, absent of the usual hustle of people and cars. Only the rhythmic clatter of German soldiers' boots and the clink of their gear against the hot tarmac broke the silence. The soldiers gathered in small groups around tanks and military trucks, poised to embark on an uncertain journey.

Just hours earlier, the streets had teemed with civilians—young women, elderly citizens—all hurrying through their routines. But when the deafening wail of sirens shattered the calm, they vanished, retreating into shelters and bunkers in a rush to prepare for the impending Allied bombings. The peace was fleeting; the drone of approaching planes soon filled the skies over Berlin.

Middle-aged mothers pressed their hands to their ears and shut their eyes, thinking of their sons on the front lines. Their only solace lay in knowing their sons believed they were serving the Reich and answering Hitler's call for a "Great Germany." His speeches stirred the elderly more than the young, as they still remembered the humiliation of the First World War. They could not forget the immense loss and suffering that followed. Few veterans could shake the memory of that defeat—the fall of the German Empire, which had once competed with the great powers of Britain and France, both of whom had outpaced Germany in securing lucrative colonies in Asia, Africa, and the Americas. Now, it was about swallowing the bitter humiliation imposed by the Allied forces after World War I.

In central Berlin, near Humboldt University, stood a building once home to middle-class Berliners. That part of the city had been a symbol of the Roaring Twenties' vibrant energy. But all the activity on the street had ceased since war was declared a year ago.

On the second floor of the Belle Époque building, Nyla struggled to breathe in the final stage of her first pregnancy. She strained to understand the news on the German State radio, her German still far from fluent. Frustrated, she turned to the Arabic-Nazi radio station. The familiar voice of Younis Bahri, an Iraqi broadcaster loyal to the Nazi regime and an admirer of Hitler, provided her with the information she sought: the war was about to engulf all of Europe. Nyla remembered meeting Bahri once at an Iraqi-themed event in Berlin. The news he shared praised Germany's advances on the front lines, especially their success in Poland.

Nyla sat uneasily in an old armchair, its worn fabric in desperate need of repair, listening to the radio's warning: Iraqi nationals were urged to leave Germany, which had declared war on the Allied forces, including Iraq, then under British control. She felt utterly alone, unable to discuss the war with anyone. Foreign nationals were under constant surveillance. Her husband, Amin, was at a lecture at Berlin University. *How could he risk it?* she thought anxiously. Suddenly, a loud knock shook the door. Breathless, she rushed over and, in broken German, called out, "Who is it?"

A faint voice replied, calm but urgent: "It's Hilda, open the door."

Relieved, Nyla struggled to unlock the heavy, fifty-year-old door. When it finally creaked open, Hilda, a white German woman in her early forties, entered, greeting her with a soft "Guten Morgen." Nyla responded first in Arabic, then in German, drawing a faint smile to Hilda's delicate lips. Dressed in a long blue dress, Hilda's weary eyes and dark circles betrayed sleepless nights, though traces of her former beauty still lingered.

"How are you holding up?" Hilda asked softly.

"I'm worried about Amin," Nyla replied, her voice trembling as much as her hands.

Hilda grasped Nyla's hand reassuringly. "Don't worry, my dear. It will be over soon."

"But why is the Arabic radio telling Iraqi nationals to leave?" Nyla muttered, raising her hands and quietly reciting verses from the Quran for protection.

"He's still here in Berlin, isn't he? He should be fine. My son, Gunter, is on the Eastern Front... I worry for him." Hilda's voice broke slightly. Nyla moved to embrace her, but Hilda gently patted her shoulder instead.

"Thank you, Hilda," Nyla said softly. "You've been with me through this entire pregnancy. I lost my mother when I was young, and after my father remarried, life was never the same. Marrying Amin changed everything. He's so bright—working on his PhD here in Germany."

Hilda smiled kindly. "Are you planning to leave Germany?"

"I don't know. I'm waiting for Amin."

A sudden, loud bang at the main gate startled them both. Nyla stood to open the door, but Hilda stopped her.

"I'll go. It's not safe for you." Hilda peered cautiously through the peephole, her body tense.

"What's wrong, Hilda?"

"It's the Gestapo," Hilda whispered urgently.

"What's that?"

"The secret police," Hilda hissed, quickly locking the door.

Nyla stared, confused by Hilda's fear. "I must hide," Hilda whispered.

"Why? What have you done?" Nyla asked, bewildered.

"I'm Jewish," Hilda confessed quietly.

The word "Jew" triggered memories for Nyla of her old school friend Eva. They had skipped school together to sneak into the local cinema, hiding beneath scarves to avoid being recognised. Growing up in Baghdad, where forty percent of the population was Jewish, Nyla had always envied Eva's freedom compared to her stricter Muslim upbringing.

Hilda had been married to a German officer during World War I. He was hailed as a hero after his early death, leaving her a widow to raise their son alone. The war pension had provided little help. Now, Hilda's voice snapped Nyla back to the present.

"Hide me, please," Hilda whispered, panic creeping in.

"Where?" Nyla asked, scanning her small two-bedroom flat. Her eyes landed on the kitchen annex, cluttered with expired food and Iraqi spices.

Before Nyla could act, another heavy knock pounded at the door. Hilda scurried to the annex, hiding as Nyla cautiously opened the door. Three blonde German officers, their uniforms spotless, stood before her. One, with a commanding tone, asked her who she was. Nyla's Middle Eastern appearance seemed to confuse them. Stammering, she tried to explain in broken German where she was from and why she was in the country.

Suddenly, a man with olive skin and a thick mustache appeared behind her, speaking in fluent but heavily accented German. "What do you want?" he demanded.

Nyla nearly collapsed, but the man caught her, holding her close. It was Amin. He explained to the officers that he was an Iraqi PhD student at Berlin University and that Nyla was his wife. Producing identification from his briefcase, Amin offered it to the eldest officer, who examined the documents with curiosity. The officer seemed to hesitate, but Amin quickly interjected.

"My wife does not speak German well, and she's pregnant. Women should tend to their families, not speak to strange men." Amin's words resonated with the younger officer, whose beliefs aligned with Nazi ideals of women's roles.

The elder officer, with a slight nod, apologised to Amin and left, followed by his subordinates. Nyla, still shaking, explained in Arabic to Amin what had transpired.

"She's Jewish," Amin whispered gravely, his fear barely contained. "We're lucky."

Hilda emerged from the annex, exhausted but grateful to be alive. Amin, with a mix of pity and urgency, offered her a way out. "We're leaving Germany in the morning. You should come with us."

"I can't leave my son," Hilda replied, her voice full of emotion.

Amin's tone was blunt but firm. "Your son is likely in a concentration camp by now, and you could be next. We have permission to leave. Come with us."

Hilda, shaken by the harsh reality, looked up at the ceiling. Could she bear to leave? Would she ever see her son again?

Chapter Two

Berlin Train Station -Lehrter Bahnhof
In the early morning, Lehrter Bahnhof Station was shrouded in tension. The train, scheduled for departure, had been delayed to avoid Allied bombing raids. The grand building, constructed in 1871 to symbolise Germany's ambition as a rising global power, now bore scars from recent attacks. Partial damage marred its once-glorious facade, and German soldiers stood watch on the remaining towers, protecting it from British air strikes.

Nyla, accompanied by her husband Amin and Hilda, approached the station with a sense of urgency. Both women wore black abayas, traditional Middle Eastern attire. Hilda, half-concealed by a khimar to hide her identity, gripped Nyla's hand tightly. Nyla, her swollen abdomen visible, deliberately emphasised her pregnancy, hoping it might garner sympathy and deflect attention from Hilda. Their appearance attracted curious glances from passers-by, as well as soldiers who eyed them warily. Foreigners were a growing concern in wartime Germany, especially as the country tightened its grip on outsiders.

With Great Britain now embroiled in the war, the British diplomatic mission in Berlin had urged its citizens and those from British protectorates, including Iraq, to leave Germany immediately, fearing imprisonment or worse. The Iraqi consulate had already shut its doors, leaving Nyla and Amin with no support as they sought to escape.

Nyla, though unused to wearing an abaya in Berlin, had brought it from Iraq. It was a garment she wore during visits to her relatives in Ana or the countryside, where customs remained conservative. Now, it was a stroke of luck that she had packed not only her own abaya but an extra for Hilda. At first, Hilda hesitated to wear it, feeling out of place. Yet she recalled that some of her Sephardic Jewish relatives had worn similar garments during religious occasions. She felt as though she had stepped back into a different era, forced to relive history in the most perilous of times.

Amin's primary concern was Nyla's safety—both hers and that of the unborn child. He wrestled with the decision to bring Hilda along, knowing the immense risk. Yet, leaving her to an uncertain fate in Nazi Germany felt unconscionable.

Hilda, after failed attempts to contact her son, had come to the sobering realisation that her life was in grave danger. The Gestapo's recent visit had only deepened her fear. Amin tried to persuade her: "There is a better chance of saving your son abroad than here in Germany."

As they reached the train inspector, Amin presented their travel documents, speaking in grammatically correct German but with a thick accent that immediately drew suspicion. "We are boarding for Baghdad," he announced.

The inspector, an elderly man drafted into service due to the younger men being sent to the front, eyed the two women with suspicion, then scrutinised the paperwork that Amin handed over. At this point, some Jews were still allowed to leave if they had foreign contacts, but they required special permission. Hilda, with her half-German, half-Jewish heritage, was at greater risk despite her father's Aryan lineage. Her darker skin and basic knowledge of Arabic, which she had picked up due to its similarity with Hebrew, added to her uneasy disguise.

Amin spoke in German. "My wife is very ill, and we Iraqis must leave immediately."

The word "Iraqi" rang strangely in the inspector's ears. He squinted, unsure whether such a country even existed. He walked over to consult with a tall, slim officer, whose approaching bootsteps sent waves of dread through Hilda. She feared it was the end, both for her and for the kind couple risking their lives to help her. Her body trembled under the silk abaya, and she fought the impulse to rip it off and scream, "I am German!"

The officer, sharp in his well-ironed uniform, arrived with an air of suspicion. He studied the scene intently before greeting them.

"Guten Morgen," he said, his tone polite but probing.

"Guten Morgen," Amin replied.

"Where are you traveling to?" the officer asked.

"To Iraq," Amin answered.

The officer's brow furrowed at the unfamiliar name. Amin clarified, "Baghdad."

The mention of Baghdad stirred a faint recognition. Perhaps the officer remembered childhood stories from *Arabian Nights*, tales his mother used to read. The officer asked for their travel documents. Amin handed him one passport, listing both him and Nyla. The officer struggled with the handwritten English details but couldn't read the Arabic script.

Noticing the women's veiled faces, the officer asked, "Why are they covered?"

Amin explained, "It is our tradition that women should not show themselves to strange men, especially not foreigners."

The officer was incredulous. "But the papers show only one woman accompanying you."

"She is my mother-in-law," Amin said quickly. "She came to help my wife with her pregnancy."

Nyla, understanding bits of the conversation, moved the abaya slightly to reveal her pregnant belly, hoping to elicit sympathy. The officer's eyes flickered, caught between duty and humanity. Before he could press further, Hilda began to cry, her sobs loud and desperate.

The officer leaned toward her. "Are you a Jew?" he asked in German.

"No," she said, her voice shaky but resolute. "I am German. My father was German, and my son is fighting for his country."

The officer glanced around to ensure no one was listening. Then, in a low voice, he warned, "Make sure to hide your identity at the borders."

Straightening up, he turned and addressed them louder, "Auf Wiedersehen," before hastily returning the documents and stepping away.

Amin wasted no time guiding Nyla and Hilda toward their carriage. As they boarded, Hilda exhaled deeply, her nerves frayed.

"I'm a wreck. That officer was a real gentleman," she whispered.

"Indeed, he was," Nyla agreed.

Once seated in their compartment, where the wooden benches were hard and uncomfortable, the train remained eerily empty of civilian passengers. Time dragged, with every minute feeling like an eternity. After what felt like hours of anxiety, the train's whistle finally blew, signalling the start of their journey.

Though the train departed the station, their unease persisted. The route would take them through German-occupied territories, and at each border checkpoint, they would need to improvise. Should Hilda feign sleep or hide in the restroom whenever officers came aboard to inspect their documents?

At one stop, a bomb from an Allied raid hit nearby, shattering the train windows and killing a civilian passenger. The train was forced to halt, and the crew struggled to contact Berlin for further instructions. The chaos from the bombing allowed Hilda to slip past several inspections unnoticed, her low profile keeping her out of danger. After days of this tense cat-and-mouse game, the train guard finally announced their arrival in Bulgaria.

Suddenly, Nyla gasped and clutched her abdomen. "Something is coming," she whispered to Hilda.

"What do you mean?" Hilda replied, alarmed.

"I think I'm in labour," Nyla cried out.

Panic spread through the compartment. Amin, wide-eyed with fear, turned to Hilda for guidance.

Hilda lifted Nyla's heavy skirt and felt the wetness seeping through. "It's time," she muttered. With no medical supplies at hand, Hilda shouted for the train inspector, breaking her silence and revealing her fluent German. Moments later, Hilda delivered the baby herself, using a kitchen knife handed to her by the inspector to cut the umbilical cord.

At the final checkpoint, as the train crossed from Nazi-occupied territory into Bulgaria, a German officer opened their compartment door to the sound of a new born baby's cries. Startled by the sight of the bloody scene and the birthing process, he quickly apologised, asking if they needed a hospital. Amin, still in shock, replied, "It's done."

The officer left, visibly shaken, as the baby let out its first wail. Hilda, wiping the new-born clean, announced, "It's a boy."

Nyla, exhausted but overjoyed, turned to Amin. "We will name him Harb."

"Harb?" Hilda tried to repeat, her voice trembling.

Amin explained, "It means war in Arabic."

The train continued, now racing toward the Turkish border. As it picked up speed, Hilda lost her balance. Amin caught her just in time, looking into her eyes—a reminder of the strength and beauty she still carried despite the war's ravages.

"Harb saved my life," Hilda whispered to herself.

Chapter Three

Turkish Delight

Hilda opened the train compartment window to catch a small dose of the early morning spring sun, just on the outskirts of the European side of Istanbul. The immense beauty of the scenery made her momentarily forget the suffocating train fumes. She hadn't fully realised the grand, prestigious appearance of the city that had once been the capital of two vast empires—the Byzantine and the Ottoman. Having grown up believing Berlin was the centre of the world, she now realised there was so much more to see and understand beyond her familiar world.

She breathed deeply, not because of the fresh air, but due to a sense of fleeting freedom. Still, guilt gnawed at her thoughts—guilt over her son's uncertain fate, suffering either in a concentration camp or fighting in a bloody war where there were no victors, only losers. It was the same plight, no matter the battlefield.

She felt hungry, having saved most of her food rations for Nyla, who needed them more due to her pregnancy and now breastfeeding. The scarcity of food had reduced their meals to Dutch Gouda cheese and dried bread, with the occasional dried meat or coffee. Amin had suggested they celebrate the birth of his son with some coffee: "Let's celebrate for our Harb," he said enthusiastically.

"With what? We barely have any food," Hilda replied, her practical mind unwilling to entertain the idea.

"In my country, people would celebrate the birth of a boy for days," Amin said with pride, meeting Hilda's astonished look. She couldn't understand why boys always seemed to take the lion's share of celebrations.

Amin led the ladies to the train's modest restaurant, where the menu, now expanded beyond simple cheese and the occasional meat stew, offered new options since crossing into Turkey. Nyla and Hilda refused to eat the meat, as it was neither halal nor kosher. Amin objected to what he saw as their overly restrictive views, insisting they were missing out on delicious food.

After crossing the Turkish border, the restaurant stocked more varieties of meat, vegetables, fruit, and sweets. The warmer climate and Turkey's neutral position in the war made food more available. Hilda, who had never strictly followed religious dietary codes, now remembered her grandmother, who had always faithfully followed Jewish dietary rules.

A young Turkish waiter reassured Nyla, "The meat is halal, madam." Amin, trying to ease Nyla's hesitation, took a piece of the meat stew and ate it. "It's halal," he said, "and she could eat kosher meat without any concerns." He glanced at Hilda, unsure of her stance, but watched as she ate her lamb stew with bread and fried eggs with a hearty appetite. No sign of repulsion appeared on her face.

After finishing their meal, they waited for tea and coffee. Suddenly, the train came to an abrupt halt. Hilda marvelled at the luxury of Turkish coffee—a precious treat during the war—and vowed not to complain about the bitter taste left by the coffee grounds. Nyla, meanwhile, craved some strong Turkish tea, which reminded her of the way her stepmother and late mother used to prepare it for breakfast and afternoon tea.

The inspector walked through the train, shouting in a tenor voice, "We are approaching Istanbul train station." The women panicked, realising they needed to pack quickly. Harb started crying, and Nyla tried to breastfeed him with her now more nutritious milk, revitalised after having a proper meal for the first time in days.

The trio, feeling heavier after their feast, struggled to reach their compartment. The meal had been too much for their nearly empty stomachs. Hilda folded her five pieces of clothing—items she had been washing and drying in the cold weather. Amin, on the other hand, carefully packed his paperwork, holding his thesis fondly. He had spent nights preparing for his research at Berlin's Pergamon Museum, focusing on the sumptuous Ishtar Gate and other Babylonian artefacts discovered by German excavations in Mesopotamia during the nineteenth century. These ancient relics had been taken to Germany in exchange for the Germans building the Baghdad railway under a deal with the Ottoman Empire. All of this had occurred before Iraq became part of the British Empire, as spoils of World War I.

Harb's cries grew louder, catching the attention of some of the few passengers aboard, who offered Nyla words of sympathy and comfort, turning her into a mini-celebrity. Her birth story became the talk of the train, offering a sliver of hope and positive news amid the bleakness of war. It was life—birth—standing in contrast to death.

The passengers on the train were few but of varied nationalities, many under the direct or indirect influence of Germany. Turkey, a neutral country, had signed a non-aggression pact with Germany. Since the German invasion of Bulgaria, Turkey had become Germany's neighbour, to the Turks' concern. President Mustafa Kemal Atatürk was determined to keep Turkey out of the war, avoiding the devastation his country had experienced during World War I. His priority was to protect the modern nation he had worked so hard to build.

Yet, German influence in Turkey was strong, and German officials closely monitored Jews fleeing their country. Hilda lived in constant terror of being caught and handed over to the Germans, knowing full well what fate awaited her if she were discovered.

The customs officer entered the train compartment, giving the two women with the new born baby a curious look. He stared at their abayas, astonished, as covering one's head had been banned in Turkey since the fall of the Ottoman Empire and the establishment of a secular republic. His initial thought was, "These Arabs are backwards," but he quickly remembered his own mother and grandmother had once worn similar attire.

When they reached the customs office, Hilda removed her headscarf, revealing her Western features, much to the officer's surprise.

Nyla, wearing a hat that functioned as a head covering in a western way, as she used to do in Germany, handed over her papers. The officer asked Hilda in the Turkish language "Are you all together?"

With steady composure and quiet resolve, she reached into her large pocket and pulled out a bundle of documents: an old passport and identification papers written in German. The officer, struggling to read the German documents, chose to let them pass rather than admit his difficulty. Turkey had allowed a few thousand European Jews to pass through to British-mandated Palestine. He was accustomed to letting people like her through, despite official instructions to scrutinise and verify if they were Jews. The presence of a family with a newborn provided Hilda with a layer of protection.

Amin struck up a conversation with the officer in Turkish. "I have Turkish ancestry," he said, trying to test the officer's nationalist sentiments.

"Really? My mother had family in Mosul," the officer responded, with a sense of pride.

Hilda, deep in her own thoughts, wondered, "Should I go back to find my son?" Her reverie was broken by Harb's cries. Nyla panicked, unsure what to do, and Hilda stepped in, showing her how to hold and burp the baby. These were skills passed down from mother to daughter, and in that moment, Hilda longed for the motherhood she had left behind. Meanwhile, Nyla wished her own mother could see her in this new maternal role, though she found some comfort in Hilda's presence.

The customs officer, reassured by Amin's Iraqi nationality, smiled and said, "My father served in the military in Baghdad during the First World War." Amin returned the smile and shook his hand warmly. They were allowed to pass safely into Turkish territory.

Amin whispered to Nyla, "Good thing he didn't bring up how the Iraqis betrayed the Turks by siding with the British back then."

Once outside, Amin walked ahead to hail a taxi to the Pera Palace Hotel in the Beyoğlu (Pera) district. As the taxi wound its way through the ancient streets, passing the fortified Sultanahmet district, Hilda commented, "It reminds me of Dresden," reminiscing about the days she worked as a housekeeper for a wealthy family in her youth.

The old Ford car reached the hotel, with little traffic on the roads, but countless people going about their business, walking indifferently toward their destinations.

The Pera Palace hotel was a belle époque masterpiece built in 1892 to cater to passengers of the Orient Express. The Ottomans had attempted to keep up with the European Renaissance movement in architecture and the arts, though they had largely been unsuccessful.

As they arrived, the porter rushed to greet them, hoping for a generous tip. Since the war had reduced the number of tourists, only wealthy refugees, exiled royals, spies, and a few Turkish officials now frequented the hotel. Hilda and Nyla observed the wealthy Turkish women, meticulously groomed with heavy makeup and hand-stitched dresses. Amin helped the porter with the luggage, surprising the man with his willingness to assist.

Inside the lavish hotel, Hilda whispered to Amin in her Berlin-accented German, "Are you sure we can afford this hotel? I could find a cheaper one downtown."

"Don't worry. The Iraqi embassy promised to cover the bill," Amin replied confidently.

"But not for me," Hilda exclaimed, her concern palpable.

"Don't forget, you're my child's grandmother," he said with a smile, revealing his white teeth beneath his dark moustache.

Amin booked two rooms, speaking in German to the receptionist, who was thrilled to have new guests. The porter eagerly led them to their rooms, hoping for a tip, which Amin gave sparingly, mindful of his limited budget. Nyla and Harb took the double room, while Hilda was shown to her single room. As she lay in bed, staring at the ornate ceiling, she marvelled, "I never dreamed I'd end up here."

She drifted to sleep, dreaming of her son and her late husband.

Chapter Four

Winds of Change

Hilda awoke early to the faint sound of the call to prayer from a small mosque nearby. The *adhan* (call to prayer in Arabic) had been banned eight years earlier by the president as part of an effort to secularise the country and sever ties with the Ottoman Empire's heritage. From her window, Hilda watched the Turkish police approach the old man calling to prayer and quietly escort him away. She didn't fully understand the significance of it all.

Despite the lingering cold of early spring, Hilda washed herself in the basin with the chilly water. She dressed in a loose, black skirt and jacket—both ill-fitting after losing weight from rationed meals and the stress of her journey. She felt the pull to explore Istanbul, a city she had read about in history books, and left a message for Amin and Nyla at the reception desk, letting them know of her whereabouts.

Hilda climbed the hill toward the historic centre, her curiosity guiding her to the magnificent Hagia Sophia. Built by the Byzantines in 537 AD and later converted into a mosque, it had since become a museum under the Turkish Republic. Across from it stood the Blue Mosque - the sight of these towering medieval structures left her in awe.

As the city came to life with the rush hour, the streets grew busier. Most of the locals were wrapped in heavy coats, and Hilda regretted leaving her old, worn coat behind, shivering against the morning chill. The scent of Turkish coffee wafted through the air, and she followed it to a man preparing coffee from a small stand.

Rummaging through her pocket, Hilda pulled out a small stash of money, hastily taken from her life savings when she fled Berlin. She had hidden the money under her living room's oriental carpet before escaping. Unsure of the exchange rate, she gestured to the coffee man, hoping he would understand.

The man chuckled, speaking passable German, "No worries, madam. Many people don't have money these days."

Hilda raised her eyebrows in surprise. "How do you speak German so fluently?"

"I used to work as a chauffeur for the German ambassador before the war. I've been to Berlin." He smiled, handing her a cup of coffee in a small china cup.

Hilda offered him a bundle of Reichsmarks, but the man waved her off. "It's on the house."

She was taken aback by his kindness, especially in such uncertain times. Sipping the hot coffee, she burned her tongue in her haste but smiled through the discomfort. After thanking the man, she continued her walk toward the Topkapi Palace, overlooking the azure blue Bosphorus.

The cold wind blew through Gülhane Park, stopping her from walking any farther. She found a bench and huddled against the wind. The park, once part of the Imperial Palace, was almost deserted. The sound of movement drew her attention to a woman sitting on a nearby bench, who was struggling to chew a piece of dry Turkish bread due to her missing teeth.

Hilda guessed the woman was likely German and approached her, offering a faint "Guten Morgen" as a greeting.

The woman, middle-aged and unkempt, responded in garbled German. Hilda sat beside her, asking, "Are you German?"

"Yes, I was. Not anymore," the woman replied, her voice filled with a resigned bitterness.

"My name is Hilda, from Berlin," Hilda said softly.

"Nice to meet you. I'm Hannah, from Hamburg."

"Do you live in Istanbul?" Hilda asked, her curiosity growing.

"For now," Hannah said with resignation, "but who knows for how long?"

Both women eyed each other with suspicion and wariness, though there was a strange connection between them. Neither was willing to reveal much, but the chemistry was palpable.

After an awkward silence, Hilda broke the tension. "I left Germany in a hurry. I'm traveling to Baghdad with a friend to help her care for her baby."

"Baghdad? That's the end of the world!" Hannah exclaimed.

"Not really, just about a week on the Baghdad Railway."

Hannah perked up. "Is it true that Jews make up forty percent of Baghdad's population?"

Hilda, cautious, replied vaguely, "I've heard that too, but I'm not sure."

Hannah's tone grew more confident. "It's better to get away from Europe these days."

"Because of the war?" Hilda tested the waters.

"Among other things. Do you think the atrocities happening in Europe are justified? Innocent people are dying for no reason," Hannah said, her voice trembling before she burst into tears.

Hilda, feeling the need to offer comfort, embraced her and whispered, "I disagree with what's happening. I'm Jewish. What about you?"

Hannah recoiled at first but then nodded. "Yes, I am. And I'm proud of it. I fled to join my husband in Mandatory Palestine, like many others. I want to belong somewhere."

Hilda, feeling the weight of her own situation, realised how fortunate she was to have escaped when she did.

Hannah continued, her voice steady despite her circumstances. "I've been in Istanbul for weeks. My money's running out, so I've been sleeping rough and relying on the local Jewish community for help."

"Are there many Jews here?" Hilda asked, now intrigued.

"Yes, quite a few," Hannah said with certainty.

"Are they doing well?" Hilda asked, subtly leading the conversation.

Hannah glanced over her shoulders to make sure no one was listening. "They've had better times. I've heard they haven't been getting along well with the Christian community. The Turkish government claims neutrality in the war, but they seem more sympathetic to the Nazis. I heard they've deported some Jews to Nazi-occupied territories. Still, they have helped others emigrate to Palestine, like my husband."

Hilda, feeling sympathy, discreetly pulled a few notes of German currency from her pocket and handed them to Hannah. Tears in her eyes, Hannah kissed Hilda's hands in gratitude. But their moment was interrupted when they saw two Turkish gendarmes walking through the park. Panic set in as they feared being detained for speaking a foreign language.

"We should leave," Hannah whispered urgently. "They'll be suspicious of us."

Hannah quickly stashed the notes into her coat pocket and hurried off. Hilda, feeling uneasy, realised she needed to return to the hotel for her own safety. She became disoriented, struggling to find her way back, when a young gendarme noticed her confusion and approached her.

He spoke in Turkish, which she couldn't understand, but his bow and gentle demeanour made it clear he was offering help.

"Pera Hotel," she said.

The young man nodded, gesturing for her to follow. As they walked in silence, Hilda's mind raced, unsure of what the future held.

Chapter Five

Tracks to the Unknown

Hilda sat at a round table with Nyla and Amin at the Hacı Abdullah Restaurant, located at the Karaköy Pier. The restaurant's owner, intrigued by the rare presence of Western tourists, came to greet them. He spoke passable German and eagerly recounted the history of the restaurant, known for serving Ottoman court cuisine in its heyday. However, he was careful to avoid over-glamorising the Ottoman era, knowing it was risky to do so in the new Republic. Turkish authorities enforced strict censorship, and speaking too fondly of the past could be problematic, especially with foreigners present.

Hilda, sensing the need to end the conversation politely, struggled to cut it short. The middle-aged manager was proud of his work, and of the generations before him, and didn't seem to want the discussion to end. But the baby's cries provided Hilda with an excuse to shift her attention, and she turned to Nyla, offering instructions on how to soothe and feed the child. Motherly instincts stirred within Hilda as she busied herself with Harb, reminding her of the days when her own son was a baby. Even though he had grown into a man, in her eyes, he would always be her little boy.

The rationing of food was evident, with their meal less abundant than a typical Turkish feast, much less the lavish fare the restaurant was known for. As Hilda scanned the menu, she was curious to try something new. Amin explained many of the dishes to her, most of which featured lamb. Though she wasn't accustomed to eating lamb, she decided to be adventurous and ordered kebabs, while Amin and Nyla opted for dolma.

"We were worried you might have lost your way earlier," Amin remarked, his voice tinged with genuine concern. He seemed to be gently broaching a conversation about the risks Hilda might face due to her behaviour.

"I'm sorry if I caused any worry. I've always dreamed of visiting this marvellous city," Hilda replied, deciding not to elaborate on her adventures. She hesitated to mention her encounter with Hannah, fearing it might alarm the couple and cause them to reconsider travelling with her.

Hilda hadn't realised how hungry she was until the food arrived. She devoured the kebabs and Turkish bread with gusto, relishing the taste of freshly baked bread soaked in a garlicky yogurt sauce. Nyla urged her to try some of the dolma, passing her stuffed vine leaves and peppers.

As they ate, a waiter brought over a bundle of newspapers, most of them in Turkish. Amin grabbed one and, though his knowledge of the language was limited, he made an effort to read it. He had learned some Turkish from his father, who had worked as a civil servant and thus had to master the language to secure a respectable job during the Ottoman rule in Iraq.

However, Amin was more comfortable with an English-language paper, a language he had mastered during his studies. Hilda, meanwhile, searched for a German newspaper. Her face grew pale, and her breathing quickened as she read the grim news about the war back home. The Nazi advances in Europe sent a chill through her, reviving memories of her childhood during the First World War.

Sensing the tension, Nyla tried to steer the conversation away from the horrors of the war. "I'm looking forward to seeing my family soon. They'll be so happy to meet my son."

The mention of the word "son" struck a chord with Hilda. "How do you say 'son' in Arabic?" she asked Amin.

"Ibn," he responded, smiling as he emulated a schoolteacher.

"Ibn," Hilda repeated softly. "It's nice, easy to say." She gazed at the baby and whispered, "Harb is my ibn too." They all laughed.

"You'll pick up Arabic in no time," Nyla encouraged her.

"I'm not sure," Hilda said timidly. "I tried learning Hebrew when I was younger, and it was difficult."

"Arabic and Hebrew come from the same language family," Amin reassured her. "It won't be as hard as you think."

"I've been trying to learn a few basic Arabic words," Hilda replied, pulling out a German-Arabic dictionary she had borrowed from Nyla.

"Don't worry," Nyla teased, "The Turks don't speak Arabic."

Hilda smiled, but Amin's next comment wiped it away. "The current Iraqi government is sympathetic to the Germans. They're Arab nationalists, trying to distance themselves from British influence."

Hilda's expression darkened. "What if they realise I'm Jewish?" she asked, her anxiety growing.

"To them, you're a German citizen," Amin assured her. "Forget your Jewish heritage for now, at least until we reach Baghdad."

Amin seemed to enjoy taking charge of their little group. He cleared his throat and announced, "We need to prepare for the next leg of our journey."

"Where are we heading?" Hilda asked.

"We'll cut through Turkey to Aleppo, in Syria," Amin replied.

Fear washed over Hilda. She knew Syria was under the control of the pro-Nazi Vichy French government. Sensing her alarm, Amin added, "You're a German citizen, remember? You'll be fine."

His attempt to calm her wasn't enough to soothe her troubled soul.

Back at the hotel, the porters brought their luggage to the reception area as they waited for a taxi to take them to the Asian terminal of Sirkeci Train Station. Once aboard the ferry, which would carry them across the Bosphorus to the eastern side of Istanbul, Harb became restless, upset by the rocking of the boat. Nyla, suffering from seasickness, was on the verge of vomiting, so Hilda took the baby, holding him tightly to comfort him and reduce the effects of the swaying boat.

The short boat ride, though brief in distance, felt interminable due to the rough sea, known for its calm waters and deep blue hues. When they finally arrived at the station, Amin hurried to secure their tickets, hiding his anxiety from the women. Missing the train would mean waiting in Istanbul for several more days, an expensive delay. Amin, a student dependent on support from his family and a scholarship, was wary of his limited funds, especially with the war complicating money transfers.

At the train station, the station manager, a man in his forties with greying hair that made him look older than his years, and wearing a black suit, greeted them warmly. He spoke fluent German, while his assistant occasionally chimed in with broken Arabic. The assistant tried chatting to the ladies but Nyla politely informed him that Hilda was an orthodox religious woman who avoided speaking with strange men. He reluctantly accepted this explanation, though not without some disappointment. He tried to explain his Arabic roots from Iskenderun in Hatay Province, southern Turkey, an area with a majority Arabic-speaking population that had long been disputed over whether it belonged to Syria or Turkey.

The station manager cut in "Welcome to the maiden voyage of the Baghdad Railway". Amin couldn't hide his excitement. He and Nyla remembered well their arduous journey from Baghdad to Beirut in an old British bus, then by sea to Italy, before continuing by train to Berlin as they had done before.

The customs officials treated them like royalty. No one inspected their travel documents or luggage. The train was nearly empty, allowing them the luxury of choosing their own compartment.

"Thanks to our clothes, they probably think we're nobility" Amin whispered to Nyla. "The Turks are probably eager to secure their share of the newly discovered oil in Mosul," he smiled with pride in his voice.

"Iraq has a 500-year history with the Ottomans," Nyla responded to show off her knowledge of history.

After a brief wait, the train began to move. The vibration of the carriage brought Hilda a sense of security. The farther she was from war-torn Europe, the safer she felt. Still, she was aware of the growing Nazi influence in the Middle East, and Syria's Vichy French government was a looming obstacle.

For now, Hilda resolved to take the journey one day at a time. Holding baby Harb in her arms, her only delight and solace, she whispered to Nyla, "How does he have such fair hair? He doesn't look like his father at all."

Nyla snickered. "Amin's father was often mistaken for an Englishman. He almost got killed in a mob during the Iraqi revolt against the British over twenty years ago."

The journey to the Syrian border would take several days, depending on the weather, the train's schedule, and, most critically, the political unrest in the regions they passed through. The four of them slept restlessly on the uncomfortable wooden seats. Their bodies ached with the stiffness from the night, and they lost count of how many unscheduled stops the train made. At least the food was better than what they had at the start of the trip, with meals featuring winter vegetables and more meat.

Hilda savoured the taste of baklava served at breakfast, alongside a strong cup of tea. Occasionally, she longed for Turkish coffee, and the train's cook, who had worked in Germany, was eager to talk at length about German culture, art, industry, and technology. Hilda reluctantly accepted the praise of the political regime, in exchange for a cup of Turkish coffee and to conceal her Jewish identity.

After several restless nights, Hilda took to sleeping on the floor. They eventually reached Adana, near the newly drawn Syrian-Turkish border. The level of anxiety rose in their compartment and Hilda overheard heated discussions between Amin and Nyla in Arabic. Though she didn't understand the language, she guessed that Amin was nervous about the risk they had taken by bringing Hilda along and worrying about their fate if the pro-Nazi authorities discovered her true identity.

She whispered to herself, "I am German through and through."

After a sleepless night on the train, they finally reached Adana. Nyla opened the window to breathe in the warm wind drifting from the Mediterranean Sea, even in the midst of winter. The train came to a halt at the newly built station.

Amin explained to Hilda that the Berlin-Baghdad railway line had been sponsored by German banks to secure access to the warm waters of the Persian Gulf and future potential colonies, competing with the British for the newly discovered oil, along with the rising imperial powers of France and Russia before World War I.

He carried the luggage and helped Nyla down from the train. Hilda followed, making her way toward the station entrance. An old man with a carriage, pulled by two tired, worn-out horses, approached them with a warm greeting. Before anyone could say a word, he hoisted the suitcases into the carriage with difficulty. Assuming they didn't speak Turkish, he tried to communicate through gestures. Amin responded in broken Turkish, asking about a reasonably priced hotel where the four of them could spend the night. The old man urged the weary horses forward, navigating through the historic city, one of the oldest continuously inhabited places in the world, until they reached the city centre and a modest, down-to-earth hotel.

The receptionist, a young man with a welcoming smile, greeted them warmly. He called to his father to announce the arrival of new guests and handed the driver a commission for bringing customers to the hotel. An elderly woman, who worked as the cleaner, led them to their rooms.

Hilda tried to give Amin some money to help cover the cost of the hotel, but he declined once again, saying, "We may need it in Baghdad."

The word "Baghdad" now felt like a distant dream. That night, Hilda lay in bed, tossing and turning between sleep and wakefulness, caught in a twilight state between Berlin and Baghdad. Her worries had shifted from thoughts of her son to concern for herself. "What will happen to me in Syria if the Nazi-backed French authorities find out who I really am?"

Question after question swirled in her mind, but eventually, exhaustion took over. After a few sips of Jägermeister—the strong German herbal spirit she had hidden in her clothes from Istanbul, careful not to offend her Muslim companions—she finally drifted off into a restless sleep.

Chapter Six

Before Crisis

The next morning, Hilda woke in the middle of the night, shouting. She looked around, realising she was not in her flat in Berlin and was actually in a hotel in Adana. It had been a nightmare. She recalled fragments of disturbed images—flashbacks that continued to haunt her throughout the day. She dreamt that she was being chased by unknown figures, running from a burning house. Her rapid breathing and heartbeat raced in an almost frantic rhythm.

The hotel porter banged on her door, shouting in Turkish, but all Hilda felt was fear and anxiety. She snapped out of her trance—caught between sleep and wakefulness, between dream and reality—at the sound of the porter insisting it was time for breakfast. She scanned the room and her gaze settled on the small suitcase she had unpacked the night before. Quickly, she rushed to the basin, washing her face with cold water and soap. As she looked into the old mirror, she realised how much she had aged over the last few months.

She took off the heavy sleeping dress she had bought in Istanbul and put on a long black dress with long sleeves. A strange, unprecedented feeling took over her—an urge to go and pray at the synagogue, as her mother had done on Saturdays. But she suppressed it. Every move needed careful calculation in these times.

A chill coming through the damaged wooden door hit her face. She had expected it to be warmer in the East than in Germany, but Istanbul had been freezing, and so was Adana. This was normal for late winter, early spring. The budget hotel couldn't afford heating, offering only a few blankets. She picked up her coat from the chair, and carried her suitcase to the door. As she opened it she heard the sound of Harb crying. She instinctively wanted to rush and comfort him, but she hesitated, reminding herself that Nyla should develop her maternal instincts and care for her child. Hilda's own son's image flashed before her eyes. Such a beautiful boy—her eyes filled with tears, but she quickly searched her coat pockets for a handkerchief to wipe them away.

With Prussian discipline, she knocked on Nyla and Amin's door, saying firmly, "I'm ready."

The bellboy rushed over, eager for a tip, but Hilda's pride kept her from handing over the suitcase. Realising that refusing might jeopardise his job, she reluctantly allowed him to take it.

Descending the old stone stairs at a measured pace, she entered the small dining area. A breakfast of strong Turkish tea, freshly baked bread, and small plates of butter, boiled eggs, salads, and honey awaited her. The hunger she had ignored the night before returned—she had refused to eat with the Iraqi couple to avoid being a burden. She counted her remaining money, uncertain if it would last through the journey to the unknown. Her Iraqi friends had been generous, covering most of the travel expenses, but her pride still stung at not being able to contribute.

An elderly woman approached slowly, her steps heavy with age. In a low tone, she whispered, "Nasilsin?" Hilda understood the woman was greeting her and nodded politely. The lady poured tea and pointed out the food on offer. Hilda nodded again and sipped the sweet, strong tea, her thoughts drifting as she contemplated the pictures on the walls, which depicted Oriental life in the old days.

She recalled the names she had heard about—Baghdad, Ali Baba, Arabian Nights—that was all she knew of the area, although Nyla had tried to explain what the city of Baghdad looked like during their coffee chats back in Berlin.

Before long, she heard a commotion from the stairs—familiar, yet incomprehensible sounds. She knew Nyla and Amin were getting ready. The bellboy was quick on his feet, eager to serve, as the war in Europe had slowed down the influx of travelers. Nyla appeared in a violet dress, warm and comfortable for the next leg of the journey. They greeted Hilda, "Guten Morgen."

She returned the greeting with a smile. Nyla was busy with the baby, trying to breastfeed him to keep him quiet, while Amin buttered a piece of bread and topped it with honey. Hilda asked for another tea and offered to hold Harb so that Nyla could eat in peace.

"You seem to have developed a taste for strong Middle Eastern tea!" Amin teased with a broad smile, showing his white teeth. "You'll fit right in with the Baghdadi society."

The hotel manager came over and greeted the group, and Amin rushed to pay the bill, so they could get on their way. The bellboy, though discontent, helped with the luggage, fearing criticism from his boss for slacking. The group boarded the carriage, and it creaked forward, pulled by two elderly, tired horses toward the station.

"Time moves slowly in the East," Hilda muttered, trying to suppress her impatience. A blend of fear and excitement churned within her as she awaited the next phase of the journey, but outwardly she remained calm and composed.

Amin, meanwhile, was lost in thought, worried about the thesis he had worked on for so long. Would he ever be able to complete his PhD now that he couldn't return to Germany? How much time and effort had already been wasted? Nyla, sitting beside him, breastfed Harb who, content with his mother's milk, was the only soul unconcerned with their troubles. Hilda smiled at him and wished she could revisit her own early childhood. It had been rough, but she had received love and care from her parents.

The morning passed slowly until the late winter sun appeared on the horizon, its warmth seeping into Hilda's body. "I feel safer for no apparent reason," she whispered to herself, the sun easing her anxiety, if only for a moment.

Chapter Seven

Critical Point

The slow steam train snaked through the green Kurd Mountains. The tortuous route caused Nyla some panic, preventing her from enjoying the spectacular scenery. Meanwhile, Hilda soaked it all in, reliving memories of her years in southern Germany and Bavaria. She recalled her father moving around the country to provide for the family. The train had to stop on several occasions—sometimes to check the engine, other times because it was too dark to continue. Although the global war hadn't reached the area yet, there was still an air of uncertainty. Turkey was neutral, though the government leaned toward the Germans. Syria, under French mandate, was divided between factions loyal to the Vichy government and the French resistance. Both the Allied and Axis powers had vested interests in the region. The ruling government was largely pro-Nazi.

The Germans had previously shown interest in oil excavation in Mesopotamia during the Ottoman rule but were pushed out by the British and French after World War I. Turkey's alleged neutrality provided some reassurance of safety, but there were no guarantees in Syria, their next destination. The borders were scrutinised, and spies from all sides roamed the area, with no apparent loyalty to any one party. Hilda could barely sleep, disturbed by the unsteady vibrations of the train, and even more so by the fear that the Nazi-allied French authorities in Syria might discover her identity. In her worst-case scenario, she'd be accused of spying for being both Jewish and German. She regretted leaving her homeland, now facing such an ordeal in a foreign land with no news of her loved ones.

"Was my decision impulsive or reasonable?"

She questioned herself repeatedly but found no answer that satisfied her. She recalled how Jewish persecution by the Nazis had begun earlier, depriving German Jews of basic rights. Yet in Germany, she was at least on familiar ground. Now, everything felt uncertain. There was no clear right or wrong, especially in war.

As the train approached Rajo in Syria, Hilda's heart began pounding. Her breathing quickened and her sweaty hands struggled to maintain a grip on her suitcase. A knock on the door of her compartment startled her. She released a faint shout in German, "Who is it?"

Nyla's soft voice replied, "It's me."

Hilda opened the door slightly and, to Nyla's surprise, hugged her tightly—an unusual display of emotion for Hilda.

"Are you okay?" Nyla whispered.

"Not really. I'm worried about what will happen if the French authorities discover me," Hilda confessed.

Nyla pulled a large black silk abaya from her bag. "That's why I came to see you." She handed the long, traditional garment to Hilda, whose confusion was evident on her face.

"What is this for?" Hilda asked, bewildered.

"You'll wear it. You'll be my conservative mother who doesn't speak or look at strange men," Nyla giggled, though Hilda didn't share her amusement.

"Wear it for now, at least until we reach Iraq. I'll wear an abaya too, and we'll blend in as two traditional women. We've done this before, remember, when we fled Germany?" Nyla reassured her with a mild smile.

"But what if they ask me questions?"

"They won't if we tell them you're my elderly mother. And if they insist, we'll say you only speak Sorani Kurdish," Nyla replied confidently.

"But what if the customs officer is Kurdish?" Hilda's cautious mind accounted for every possible scenario.

"They won't be. The Kurdish dialect here is different from the one in Iraq. I can say my father is Arab, and my mother is Kurdish," Nyla assured her.

"You think that'll work?" Hilda asked, still unsure.

"Trust me. Amin and I have thought this through. After all, they're not supposed to speak to a respectable, religious woman," Nyla added, as she left Hilda's compartment.

Nyla, feeling proud of her plan, returned to her own compartment, where she began applying makeup, starting with kohl to line her eyes. "I need to look fresh," she said, giving Amin a flirtatious glance.

Amin kissed her cheek and pulled her close to his muscular chest, but then quickly urged her to get ready, adding "Don't forget about the baby." Nyla let out a faint, teasing laugh as she prepared herself for the journey ahead.

The train eventually stopped, its passengers shaken as they hurried to disembark at the customs station in Rajo. They were greeted by a small, old Ottoman-style building, with French government officials' photos adorning the walls. The head of staff, a French officer, sat at the centre of the office, surrounded by Syrian staff that seemed submissive and waited for his command.

The lines for customs were segregated by gender, with a separate line for families. Hilda struggled to keep hold of the slippery fabric of her abaya, which repeatedly slid from her sweaty, shaky hands. She had no experience wearing such garments, and it showed. Covering most of her face, she left only a small opening to see through, as traditional women did. Nyla kept referring to Hilda as "mother" in both Arabic and Kurdish, hoping to reinforce their story. The young customs clerk approached Amin, ignoring the women out of respect, as was customary. Amin explained that his mother-in-law was ill and needed to sit down.

The clerk rushed to bring a chair for Hilda. Amin handed over their passports, explaining that the elderly woman was traveling on her daughter's passport. Confused, the clerk approached his superior, the French officer, handing over the paperwork with deference. The French officer raised his eyes, scrutinising the group. He was more suspicious of Amin than the women. An Iraqi who had studied in Germany and was now fleeing the war? And with two traditionally dressed women? It all added to his conundrum.

The officer instructed the young clerk to bring Amin into his office. He spoke in French, but Amin responded in both German and English, trying to reassure him. Amin explained his background, his studies in Germany, and his PhD thesis on the history of Mesopotamia, which intrigued the officer. He recalled visiting the Louvre with his father and gazing at the Babylonian Code of Hammurabi.

The two became engrossed in a conversation about history and culture, until baby Harb's cries interrupted them, providing an unexpected lifeline.

"It was nice talking with you. I'm sorry but the baby's distressed from the journey," Amin said apologetically.

The French officer stood up, bowed slightly, and handed back the documents without opening them. Hilda exhaled a sigh of relief, then looked at the baby and whispered to herself, "Once again, you've saved my life."

Chapter Eight

Time in Aleppo

The train reached the ancient city of Aleppo—Halab, as it is called in Arabic—just before sunset. The new train route was desperately needed to restore the city's previous importance and strategic position between east and west, where the ancient Silk Road once passed through its old citadel centuries ago. Aleppo had lost much of its commercial significance after the opening of the Suez Canal in 1860 and the discovery of new trade routes that bypassed the old ones, cutting out European middlemen and their costly commissions.

The trio looked forward to seeing this ancient city, once the third-largest in the Ottoman Empire after Istanbul and Cairo, before it was taken over by the French after the First World War. As they disembarked, tired and old horses awaited them, the drivers eagerly competing for clients. One driver grabbed their luggage before Amin could agree on a fare, forcing him to follow, with the women behind him. They tried to calm baby Harb, who was crying loudly, but the swinging of the carriage on the unpaved road worked like a cradle, soothing him into silence.

As the carriage rattled along, the old driver began explaining the history of the city's ancient citadel, surprising Amin with his knowledge. He had assumed the man was illiterate. The roads became narrower as they approached the centre, transforming into alleyways where the carriage struggled to pass. The customs officer had recommended a small, cheap hotel in the city centre, but the driver insisted he knew better, dismissing the Damascus-based clerks as clueless about Aleppo, where he had been born and raised. His accent reminded Nyla of her late father, who had spoken similarly, having grown up in western Iraq when Syria and Iraq were still one country.

Amin took on the role of teacher, explaining to the women how the Aleppo accent resembled that of western Iraq and Mosul, owing to the region's shared history with the Hamdanid Dynasty in the 10th century. Hilda, however, could make no distinction between the people's looks, accents, or dress; to her, they all seemed the same.

The carriage finally stopped in front of an old hotel, three stories tall, with narrow, slippery stairs smoothed by time. Hilda held baby Harb in her strong arms, noticing Nyla's fearful expression at the prospect of carrying him up the stairs. The driver, despite his age and frail appearance, hauled the luggage with surprising strength, declining Amin's offer to help with immense pride. The receptionist was overjoyed to book two rooms for his rare guests. He mentioned that the Baghdad Railway Company had announced the train would depart for Mosul in a day or two.

Amin, now embodying a macho persona, announced decisively, "Let's freshen up and then go out for a meal." The women looked at him in astonishment at his sudden assertiveness, at odds with his usual behaviour in the West. Hilda entered her room, struggling to open the rusty door. The room was bare except for a bed with clean sheets and an old wooden wardrobe. She checked the sheets, distrusting the cleanliness of the hotel. She opted to leave her belongings in her suitcase, unsure when they would depart, as the train company used the war in Europe as an excuse for service delays. She washed her face, neck, and armpits in cold water from the stony basin, although she longed for a hot bath. She changed her underwear, put on the same dress, and gazed out the window at the dimly lit streets, watching vendors pack up for the day.

A gentle knock at the door startled her. It was Amin, asking, "Are you ready for the meal?" Hilda replied, "I'll be down in a minute." She hurried to put on her hat and descended to the lobby, where Amin waited. He led the group with a newfound desire to show off his knowledge, explaining Aleppo's rich history as they rode through the city. Nyla, more focused on calming her son, paid little attention, while

Hilda listened to the soothing sound of horse hooves on the uneven road.

They arrived at a small restaurant downtown, recommended by the hotel owner. The group was welcomed warmly and ushered to the family section, separate from the single men's area. The owner greeted Amin but avoided acknowledging the women, while the waiters gazed at Hilda's Western appearance in amazement. Feeling conscious of their stares, she quickly covered her face with her abaya.

The waiter addressed Amin, ignoring the women, and offered a variety of local dishes: hummus bi tahina, foul, and kubba. Amin requested lamb kebab, which he missed after their time in Turkey. He praised his late mother's kubba, to Nyla's slight discomfort. The meal arrived, properly arranged on a large tin tray. Nyla explained to Hilda, "Kubba is made from cracked wheat dough stuffed with minced lamb, herbs, spices, and sometimes nuts, while hummus is chickpeas with sesame paste."

"I'll try my luck," Hilda said, examining the food with a puzzled expression. She dipped a piece of bread into the hummus, searching for a fork and knife but finding only a spoon. Glancing at the family on the next table, she saw them eating with their hands and decided to do the same, much to the surprise of her hosts, who followed suit. At first, the taste was unfamiliar, but hunger made the food delicious.

Amin encouraged her to try the meat, pushing the plate toward her. "I know you Germans are meat eaters."

"I grew up in a poor Jewish family during the First World War. There wasn't much meat on the dinner table," Hilda replied with a smile.

They ate and laughed, momentarily forgetting the war and its horrors. After the meal, they enjoyed dessert—kunafa (vermicelli stuffed with cheese and soaked in syrup). Hilda wished for more, savouring every bite.

As they washed down the meal with black tea, a small Peugeot truck pulled up, and a French officer, accompanied by two scruffy Syrian soldiers, entered the restaurant. The officer, slim and muscular in his elegant uniform, marched toward them. The trio felt a wave of fear. They wished they had stayed at the hotel.

The officer saluted them in French, his eyes scrutinising Hilda. Nyla quickly wrapped half her face with a scarf, while Amin stood to face him.

"I need to check your papers," the officer said in a polite but firm tone, his gaze fixed on Hilda.

Amin fumbled through his briefcase, finally producing a bundle of papers and passports. "We are Iraqis. These are for me and my family," he said in broken French, a language he had tried to learn during his brief time working with a French excavation mission in Iraq.

The French officer, intrigued by Amin's French, relaxed slightly. "Is this your family?" he asked.

"Yes, my wife and her mother. They are traditional women and do not speak to strangers."

The officer bowed politely and motioned for his soldiers to move on. The trio exhaled in relief, their fears momentarily quelled.

Chapter Nine

Feeling Safe

The warm, golden rays of the sun felt blinding against Hilda's light-coloured eyes as she woke up, groggy from a restless night. She had struggled to sleep, haunted by nightmares of being detained and sent to a concentration camp. Jolted awake, she rushed to the old stone basin, struggling to turn on the rusty tap. Cold water splashed on her pale face, refreshing her and pulling her back to reality.

She longed to explore the old Citadel of Aleppo but couldn't wait to leave for Baghdad, as her fear of the unknown took precedence. Hilda's instinct was to flee immediately, her anxiety making it hard to distinguish between survival instincts and sheer panic. She quickly dressed in her dark blue travel gown with long sleeves, paired with a white headscarf Amin had bought her from the local market. Her suitcase, still unpacked, sat in the corner of the room, a constant reminder that they could need to leave at any moment. With a sigh of relief, she reassured herself that everything was ready for a quick departure.

Amin had mentioned that the train to Baghdad might depart the next morning, or perhaps the day after. The station wardens offered no certainty: "You have to wait at the station," they repeatedly told him when he inquired. The contrast between the East and the West couldn't have been more pronounced. In Germany, the train schedules had been precise, while here, uncertainty seemed to rule.

Hilda opened her door and was startled to find Nyla already standing outside, wearing a light pink dress that revealed a glimpse of her cleavage on her slim frame. Her dark hair flowed past her shoulders, matching the colour of her chestnut eyes. Hilda couldn't help but think how striking she was. Nyla rushed over, greeting her with, "Good morning! Did you sleep well?"

"Not really... I can't wait to leave this city," Hilda whispered, her last words barely audible. She remembered Amin's warnings about speaking too openly in public and quickly scanned the area to make sure no one else was around.

"We're ready," Nyla replied, heading back to her room, where baby Harb was already crying for his morning feed.

Hilda offered to help pack, only to find that Amin and Nyla were far more organised than she had expected. She had assumed that people in the East were more disorganised compared to her German standards, but this was clearly not the case. As they finished packing, a porter arrived with a tray of hot tea, freshly baked bread, sheep cheese, and honey. Hilda's eyes lit up at the sight of Baklava, which she had come to adore throughout their journey in Turkey and Syria.

"It's not typical to serve Baklava for breakfast," Nyla said, glancing at the tray in surprise.

Hilda nibbled on a small piece, while Amin helped himself to the rest.

The porter loaded their suitcases into an old French Citroën, and they squeezed inside with their luggage. As the car crawled towards Aleppo station, each second felt like an eternity to Hilda. Her eagerness to leave the city grew by the minute, hoping to avoid any more unexpected events.

The station was small, with a single platform. A train warden blew his whistle fiercely, as if trying to terrorise the passengers into action, despite the train showing no signs of movement. It seemed like a performance, a display of authority over the helpless passengers whose patience was wearing thin. After what felt like an endless wait, the train's engines sputtered to life, filling the air with smoke and noise.

They rushed on board with baby Harb wailing in competition with the whistle's shriek. Porters scrambled to grab their suitcases, each hoping for a tip. Amin handed a few Syrian pounds to the oldest porter before they entered their carriage. To Hilda's surprise, this train was much older than the one they had boarded in Berlin.

They settled into a large compartment, their belongings quickly scattered around. Harb's toys and clothes seemed to take over the small space, much to Hilda's dismay. She shot Nyla an irritated look before starting to organise everything herself. The inspector knocked on the door and waited for permission to enter, aware that there were women inside. His eyes briefly met Amin's before respectfully avoiding the ladies. Hilda, now well-practised in covering her face, played the part of a proper senior Muslim woman, blending into her surroundings to avoid attracting attention.

While Nyla changed Harb's diaper, Amin checked their tickets and paperwork. Hilda busied herself organising the luggage, avoiding any interaction with the inspector. She had seamlessly slipped into the role of grandmother, offering Nyla advice on how to feed and care for the baby. Though her tone was often bossy, Nyla took her advice gratefully, appreciating Hilda's presence as a stand-in for her late mother.

Suddenly, a cacophony of boots and shouting echoed through the train's communal passage, blending French and Arabic into an unintelligible blur. A loud knock on the compartment wall sent a wave of panic through the group, though Harb's cries, rising in intensity, masked some of the tension.

The door opened to reveal a middle-aged French officer, impeccably dressed, followed by two younger Syrian soldiers in scruffier uniforms.

"Are you Iraqis?" the officer barked without pleasantries.

"Yes, we are," Amin replied in his soft, heavily accented French.

The French language seemed to soften the officer's demeanour, as did Harb's wails.

"You came from Berlin?" he asked, switching to German.

"Yes," Amin confirmed.

"And what were you doing in Germany?"

"I was studying history at the University of Berlin," Amin said calmly.

"We have information that a German woman is traveling with you. We need to verify that." The officer's tone grew sterner, determined to uncover the truth.

Amin quickly realised the lie about Hilda being his mother-in-law wouldn't hold up under scrutiny. He stepped closer to the officer and, in a calculated gamble, whispered theatrically, "We are on a mission."

He knew he was taking a risk, but also knew that Germany's growing ties with Iraq's government, under the newly appointed Prime Minister Rashid Ali al-Gaylani, which opposed British control, might work in their favour. The German-Arabic radio broadcasts by the Palestinian dissident Haj Amin al-Husseini, who had sought refuge in Berlin, were well known across the Arab world.

"We are friends," Amin whispered into the officer's ear.

The officer's eyes scanned the compartment, trying to discern which of the women was the German. Hilda didn't hesitate. She removed her veil, revealing her Western features, and spoke in fluent, if slightly accented French, "It's me, sir."

The officer hesitated, his confusion evident. Hilda added, "We cannot reveal more, sir. Please, excuse us—the baby needs feeding." Right on cue, Harb began to wail again. Nyla uncovered her breast to feed him, and the two Syrian soldiers, embarrassed, quickly left the compartment.

The officer, now convinced that Hilda was no refugee but part of a secret mission, saluted the group politely and left.

The trio let out a collective sigh of relief. Moments later, the train's whistle blew again, signalling its departure. They burst into laughter, tension melting away. Hilda looked down at baby Harb and said with a smile, "Thank you. You've saved me again."

Chapter Ten

En route to Mosul

The trip to Mosul took a day and night with only a few stops along the way. Nyla and Amin took turns napping whenever the baby was asleep. They also shared the responsibility of calming Harb, who was unsettled by the changes in both the environment and the temperature—things beyond his comprehension. The stress of traveling had made him more irritable, and Hilda shared in that mood. At times, the rocking of the train would lull him to sleep like a cradle, but on other occasions, it startled him awake from his baby-deep slumber.

Hilda, too, struggled to rest, staying alert in anticipation of any unexpected events. She tried to stifle her yawns behind her hand, her eyes heavy but unrelenting. Despite her lingering anxiety from recent events in Aleppo, she felt a growing confidence that her story was convincing enough to keep her safe. Still, she feared what might happen if pro-Nazi officials discovered her Jewish background. The warm sunlight streaming through the wooden window glass, mixed with a crisp, cold draft, kept her alert. There was no heating on the train, so she wrapped herself in layers of blankets for warmth.

The arrival of the bellboy with a tray of warm tea and baklava thrilled Hilda, who eagerly sampled the new treat. Amin explained the historical connection between the desert and the Ottoman sultans as Hilda nibbled on the sweet pastry, washing it down with noisy sips of tea. She realised she hadn't eaten in what felt like ages. The conductor's voice, still reassuring, announced their approach to Mosul, though the exact time of arrival remained unclear as hours passed without sight of the city.

Hilda found herself captivated by the changing landscapes. From the green mountains of Turkey to the rolling hills between Aleppo and Mosul, the scenery seemed endless. She marvelled at how it matched descriptions of paradise in the Bible.

"You missed the best part last night," Amin exclaimed, snapping her out of her daydream.

"Which part?" she responded, feigning an eagerness to learn from him.

"The landscape—spectacular old cities dotted around. Soon, we'll pass Hamam al-Alil with its natural hot springs, known for their healing powers."

"Like Baden-Baden in Germany?" Hilda interrupted, "Though I doubt they have the same medicinal properties."

Amin, encouraged by her response, continued, "We'll also pass the ruins of Nimrud, once the capital of the Assyrian Empire."

Though not well-read, Hilda recognised some of these biblical names from her early childhood, when she would read the Old Testament at the synagogue with her mother. She had been forced to reduce her attendance after the Nazis came to power, to avoid drawing attention to her background.

She looked in awe out of the window at the massive Assyrian monuments, as Amin proudly recited stories of ancient history. His enthusiasm was undeterred by Nyla's repeated calls for help with their increasingly distressed child. Hilda's mind wandered as she recognised some of the statues from Berlin's Pergamon Museum. Undaunted, Amin launched into a detailed explanation of the differences between Babylonian, Sumerian, and Assyrian artefacts, his excitement akin to spotting a wild animal in its natural habitat rather than in a zoo. Hilda had flashbacks of taking her bored son to see the Ishtar Gate at the museum in Berlin.

Suddenly, the conductor's voice rang out, roughened from overuse: "We are approaching Mosul!"

Amin stopped his lecture and turned to Hilda. "Are you still with me?"

"Sorry, I'm listening. It's just a lot to take in for someone like me."

Before Amin could reply, the train jolted to a sudden stop, throwing passengers and luggage around the cabin. Hilda and Amin rushed to gather their belongings, while Nyla focused on calming Harb.

At the station, the staff lined up, the managers dressed in hand-stitched suits and the porters in shabby uniforms. It felt like a royal reception for the first train from the continent to arrive at their newly built station. Amin couldn't resist offering more knowledge. "This is the city of two springs," he announced.

"Why is it called that?" Hilda asked.

"Because it has both a winter and a summer spring. There's no autumn here—just beautiful nature and endless history."

As they descended from the train, Hilda was struck by the lush green landscape, so different from the desert she had expected. They passed through customs, where a young, sleep-deprived clerk in a wrinkled suit processed their passports after a brief conversation with Amin. Upon noticing the two traditionally dressed women with a noisy baby, he quickly ushered them through without further delay.

After leaving the station, they boarded an old Anglia car that emitted suffocating fumes. The blond-haired taxi driver, with a stiff, almost British-like demeanour, saluted them. Nyla, eager to show she also had some knowledge, noted, "This place is a melting pot of races, part of the ancient Silk Road."

Amin directed the driver to take them on a detour through the city, keen to share more of Mosul's history. As they passed the remains of the ancient city wall and the famous Nabi Younis Mosque, Nyla expressed her desire to visit the site and pray for their safety. The car continued through the city, which was encircled by the remnants of a massive stone and mudbrick wall dating back to around 700 BC. Hilda admired the grand arches and gates, remnants of Nineveh's former glory, and the eternal Tigris River surrounded by green hills.

Eventually, they arrived at a narrow street where only bikes, donkeys, and pedestrians could pass. The taxi driver insisted on carrying the luggage and as he walked further, they passed many doors that all looked similar. He stopped at one with a handwritten Arabic sign. Amin read it and realised it was a hotel. The driver knocked on an intricately carved door, which was opened by an old woman who quickly covered her face upon seeing the male stranger, but let her veil down when she saw two women and the taxi driver who was probably a relative of hers.

The old woman led them upstairs to two adjacent rooms, separated by a thin wall that offered little privacy. After paying the young driver his fare and a tip, Amin explained to the ladies that they would need to stay for a few days, as the train service to Baghdad was delayed due to a track issue. Most local resources were being diverted to the war effort, with trains primarily used to transport British troops and munitions. Amin assured them he would visit the station daily for updates.

"Let's freshen up and grab a meal," Amin suggested.

Hilda, exhausted, lay down on the uncomfortable wooden bed and fell asleep immediately. When she woke to the sound of the Muslim call to prayer, followed by church bells, she felt as though a new chapter of her life was beginning. There was a knock at her door, and she pulled herself from the bed's sagging springs to answer it. Nyla stood there, smiling warmly.

"How are you? I'm sorry I haven't spent much time with you," Nyla said, her voice timid.

Hilda gazed at her seriously. "We've been together almost constantly."

"I know, but you've seemed... distant," Nyla replied, searching for the right words.

"I've been worrying about my son," Hilda admitted, her voice breaking as she burst into tears.

Nyla moved forward and hugged her. "Now that I have a son, I understand."

Hilda, wanting to change the subject, said, "We haven't had a proper bath in ages."

Nyla's face lit up. "Mosul is famous for its communal baths. I'll arrange for Amin to take care of Harb and we will spend the whole day at a hammam."

"A whole day?" Hilda asked, astonished.

"Yes, it's a social event here, where women not only bathe, get massages, and scrub their bodies, but also enjoy some talking therapy," Nyla giggled.

Hilda smiled, processing the new information.

"Let's hurry—Harb's probably hungry." Nyla dashed out, alarmed by her son's cries and her husband's struggle to soothe him.

Hilda glanced at the contents of her suitcase, still not quite understanding why Middle Eastern women made such an event out of bathing, requiring special clothes and accessories. To her, it was simply about getting clean. She searched for more modest clothes to cover her shoulders and arms, wondering if her light summer dress—the only one she managed to pack hastily while fleeing her homeland—would be appropriate.

Since the unrest and rising anti-Semitic sentiment in Germany, Hilda, like many Jewish women, had kept a suitcase packed in case they needed to flee or were sent to concentration camps. She never would have dreamed she'd end up in this part of the world. The furthest east she had ever been was the Pergamon Museum in Berlin, where she had marvelled at the massive monuments of Babylon and the Middle East. Now, she was living out a dream that had derived from misfortunate events. She searched for clean underwear, hanging the freshly washed ones to dry, refusing to let the chambermaid handle her clothes, feeling that this was something personal only she should do.

A heavy knock startled Hilda. In broken Arabic, she called out, "Enter." The door opened, and Amin stepped in. Hilda stood up straight.

"I hope you're feeling well," he said in a soft tone.

"I'm fine, thank you. But I do miss home," Hilda replied, switching to German with her distinct Berlin accent, needing to express herself to someone who understood.

"I know what you mean. I've been there," Amin said sympathetically. "However, I've arranged a tour of the city for you before you and Nyla go to the public bath. I'll look after Harb."

"Thank you. I don't know how to express my gratitude for you and your wife saving my life," Hilda said, her voice sincere.

Amin smiled broadly, his thick moustache framing his handsome, long face, before he left the room.

Nyla entered, looking relieved to be free of baby duty for a while. "Let's go. What a relief to finally take care of ourselves! It can be so exhausting looking after others all the time," Nyla said, showing a brief glimpse of her selfish side.

Chapter Eleven

Feeling Like a Tourist

Hilda and Nyla rushed down the hotel stairs to meet the driver, eager to follow Amin's plan, but they had their own agendas as well. The horse-drawn carriage waiting for them was impeccably clean. Its driver, a middle-aged man who looked older than his years, showed the toll of the sun on his fair skin. Two elderly horses pulled the carriage through the narrow streets of the old city, past historic landmarks like the Nabi Younis mosque and the Al-Nuri Mosque, with its famous 11th-century leaning tower known as *al-Hadba* or *the hunchback*. The tour ended at the 9th-century ancient church, Shamoun Al-Safa, after passing by the magnificent Sasson Synagogue in the Jewish quarter.

Hilda held her breath, captivated by the awe-inspiring architecture dating back over a thousand years and the remarkable religious diversity of the area. For the first time, she felt a yearning to pray, to find some inner peace amidst the emotional storm swirling inside her. Sensing the shift in Hilda's demeanour, Nyla spoke gently.

"I understand your need to worship, Hilda."

"My family is secular to the core, but I feel the need to escape, just for a moment, from the harshness of reality," Hilda admitted, her words tumbling out.

Nyla seized the moment to offer reassurance.

"I get it. Amin mentioned that there's growing anti-British sentiment here in Iraq, more sympathy towards the Germans. People don't want to be controlled by the British anymore, not since the first World War. And there's increasing discontent with the Jewish immigration to Palestine. Many Arabs are unhappy with the idea of a Jewish state."

Hilda was taken aback by Nyla's words. She had never heard anything like it before.

"I'm a German Jew—that's all. And more of the latter, really," she replied, slightly shaken.

Nyla, more informed by current events, was already aware of the Zionist movement's efforts to establish a Jewish state in Palestine after the Balfour Declaration. The two women exchanged puzzled looks, both struggling to grasp the complexities of the political situation. Though they came from vastly different backgrounds, they shared a bond like that of a mother and daughter, looking after one another. Setting aside their confusion, they chose to carry on with their journey.

The driver's loud "Hooo" signalled their arrival at their destination, a communal bath near the old public hospital. An elderly woman greeted them in a distinct Mosul Arabic accent, more classical and authentic than the Baghdadi dialect, which had absorbed many foreign words over time. Hilda was mesmerised by the bathing customs. The old woman offered them a pink-coloured drink, which made Hilda hesitate. She shot Nyla a questioning glance.

"It's pomegranate juice," Nyla explained, reassuring her.

Hilda took a cautious sip, the sweet juice reviving her as she prepared for the bathing rituals ahead. They were led to a seating area cushioned with clean pillows, separated by a muslin curtain from other women who were chatting—some about their husbands and children, others about the rising cost of living during the war and the scarcity of essentials like tea and sugar. A few discussed the recent political changes and the possibility of a new government.

Curious, Hilda considered joining the conversation but noticed Nyla's indifferent expression and decided against it. When they finished their refreshments, the attendant led them to the changing rooms and handed them heavy towels—a clear sign to undress. The women exchanged hesitant glances, unsure whether to part company. Their dilemma was solved when the elderly attendant returned, handing them blocks of Aleppo soap and body scrubbers.

"I'll start with the older lady," she announced, pointing to Hilda, who understood without translation.

"I think you should go with her," Nyla whispered with a hint of amusement.

Reluctantly, Hilda removed her clothes, her eyes scanning her sagging body, though the bath attendant praised her appearance. She found Hilda exotic and, after attempting to converse with her in Arabic, turned to Nyla for clarification.

"She's mute," Nyla whispered to the attendant.

"Is she from here or the north? Her fairness suggests she's from the north," the woman mused.

"She is," Nyla replied curtly, eager to end the conversation. She covered her semi-naked body, aware that the older women in the bath would have preferred to see their sons marry plumper, healthier women, not someone as slender as herself.

The bath attendant led Hilda into the steam room, where visibility was limited by the thick vapour. She gestured for Hilda to lie on a marble bench and rinsed her with warm water. The warmth eased the aches in Hilda's back, and she began to relax as the attendant scrubbed her body vigorously with a rough loofah, even using volcanic stones to slough off the dead skin on her heels. Though the process was painful, especially after restless nights spent on hard train seats, the final rinse of hot water felt heavenly.

Wrapped in towels, Hilda returned to the seating area, glancing around for Nyla. She spotted her, still immersed in the cleansing process, her skin glowing from the layers of dead skin that had been scrubbed away. Nyla soon joined her, beaming.

"How was it?" Nyla asked, her voice bright and energised.

"I feel like a huge weight has been lifted off my shoulders," Hilda replied, laughing. For the first time in a long while, she felt at peace.

"Let's get dressed. The weather is so fresh—spring-like. Mosul is known for its pleasant spring weather, though it also experiences long summers and short, harsh winters. Amin told me King Ghazi's Garden is spectacular, full of beautiful flowers. He'll take care of the baby, and we'll have a day out, like German women do," Nyla said, a spark of excitement in her eyes.

"German women are too serious to have fun these days. But who is King Ghazi?" Hilda asked, curious.

"He was the Iraqi monarch, but he came from Mecca, in Hejaz. Actually, the British appointed his father, Faisal I, as King of Iraq after World War I, when the Arab-speaking countries were divided between Britain and France. King Ghazi died in a car accident, but many believe it was a plot by the British-affiliated government and intelligence because of his anti-British stance."

Hilda's eyes widened at the new information, and she muttered to herself, "There's not much fairness in the world."

Feeling refreshed, they left the *hamam* and climbed back into the waiting carriage. Nyla instructed the driver, "To King Ghazi Gardens, please."

Chapter Twelve

Final Destination

The trio boarded the morning train to Baghdad. The Mosul stop brought them a refreshing pause, especially for Hilda and the new born baby. Surrounded by a large Jewish community, Hilda felt less concerned about Nazi sympathisers and looked forward to the even greater Jewish presence awaiting them in Baghdad. Yet, her heart remained in Berlin, her mind preoccupied with thoughts of her homeland and her people. Despite everything, she still considered herself German first.

As they travelled, the three openly discussed the train's quality, noting how its seats and services paled compared to the Berlin-to-Istanbul line—apart from the delicious food. They attributed the difference to the war, which had diverted resources to British troops and reduced the number of travellers. The journey took a day and a half, with various stops along the way, crossing the Tigris at multiple points and moving from lush green landscapes to stretches of desert.

Hilda had hoped to explore many of the sights they passed. An inspector, keen on local history, informed them that work on the Berlin-Baghdad railway extension to Basra was progressing. Hilda and Nyla did not share his enthusiasm, but enjoyed the absence of the scrutiny they'd faced earlier in their journey. Gazing out the window, Hilda took in the changing landscape—from mountains to agricultural fields and finally to the vast desert. She marvelled at the immense wheat fields, remembering lessons her father taught her about the Sumerians, the first to cultivate the crop. She never dreamed she'd visit the land of the Jewish prophet Ezekiel, which her rabbi had taught her about as a child. Her father had also told her about the Jewish diaspora and how they had moved from Eastern Europe to Germany centuries ago. To Hilda, she felt deeply connected to that history.

The desert was a complete novelty to Hilda, and she was more mesmerised by the fact that each city told a story of that ancient land, from the Sumerians, Persians, Assyrians, Akkadians, Arabs, Mongols, and Turks to its current form as a newly crafted British territory. Amin attempted to summarise five thousand year of history in a short trip.

"Beyond all that historic glory and stunning architecture, there must have been people who suffered greatly," Hilda remarked.

Amin ignored her comment; the plight and sacrifices of those who built those immense monuments had never occurred to him. He continued eagerly recounting his knowledge of empires and kings.

"You'll be even more impressed when you visit Babylon and the Ziggurat of Ur down south," said Amin. But he soon noticed Hilda's mind drifting away, sensing she was preoccupied with thoughts of her homeland and her son's fate.

Observing Nyla breastfeeding, he bent down to kiss his son on the forehead, despite his wife's gentle objections, for fear of disturbing the baby. Hilda watched their loving exchange, reminded of her son's father, a young German man she'd met while working at a Berlin textile factory. They'd fallen in love and dreamed of marriage, but both families disapproved of their union.

The memories flooded back to her, as vivid as ever. She remembered her mother's words, "How could a Jew and a Christian German be together?"

"But we've been Germans for centuries," Hilda had replied, her eyes welling with tears.

"Dear, we are what we are," her mother had replied, "His family won't approve, and what would I tell the Jewish community?"

Hilda and Gunter had enjoyed the freedom of the Weimar Republic, celebrating together after long shifts. One night, after a few drinks, she had accompanied Gunter to his room, both overcome with an intense need to be close to each other. She could still feel the warmth of that night, a memory that lingered, though Gunter later left for better opportunities in Bavaria. The letters had eventually dwindled, and her mother soon noticed the changes in her daughter's body. By then, Hilda's pregnancy was undeniable, and her mother arranged for her to give birth in a Bavarian monastery.

Gunter became a memory, while her son became her reality. As anti-Semitic sentiment rose in Germany, she focused on raising him alone. Lost in these memories, Hilda began to cry. Nyla noticed and approached, placing a comforting hand on her shoulder. "What is it, Hilda?" she asked softly.

"It's my son, Nyla," Hilda replied, her voice breaking. "I don't know what's become of him."

"It's God's will," Nyla replied, echoing words she'd heard from her grandmother after her mother's early death.

"Is it God's will to uproot people, to torture them, to deprive them of those they love?" Hilda's voice was laced with sarcasm and disbelief.

Nyla frowned slightly. All her life she had learned to cope with hardship by adopting such a philosophy, accepting hardship and awaiting rewards in the next life.

They spent the night eagerly anticipating their arrival in Baghdad. Hilda fell asleep, dreaming of a reunion with her son, only to be jolted awake by the inspector's announcement: "We are approaching Baghdad."

Chapter Thirteen

At Last, Baghdad

The train finally pulled into the newly built Baghdad station, a grand and imposing structure designed to impress travellers from glamorous cities like Berlin. This was one of the first trains to arrive since the rail line's inauguration, and the station manager stood tall, like a representative of Iraq's king, surrounded by clerks, sweepers, and a small crowd of families eagerly awaiting loved ones.

The station staff took pride in this advanced marvel of technology, reconnecting the long-forgotten city of Baghdad with the rest of the world. Train whistles filled the air, mingling with engine fumes and disrupting the fresh, lovely atmosphere of early spring. The head station inspector blew his silver whistle to clear the bustling crowd, establishing his authority. As the train came to a halt, flag-waving wardens signalled to the driver to mark the journey's end, though it was hardly necessary. When the doors opened, passengers were eager to disembark after days confined in the wooden and iron compartments. Despite the inspector's calls to take it slow, people urged forward, ready to reunite with loved ones. Station porters rushed toward the crowd, hoping to earn a bit of income by carrying luggage.

An elderly porter with a thick, unkempt grey beard and a strong Karada accent proudly declared his connection to this part of Baghdad, known as the original "round city," founded by the Abbasid caliph Al-Mansour in 762 AD. Though his frame was feeble, he carried heavy luggage with surprising strength. Amin waited for Nyla to exit with the baby held firmly in his arms, ensuring his safety, while Hilda firmly declined the porter's offer to carry her bags which were light enough for her to carry. Bright golden sunlight momentarily blinded her, while the scent of orange blossoms mingled with train fumes and pierced her senses. She was both bemused and excited by the noisy, chaotic flow of the bustling crowd. It felt like stepping into a wonderland from her childhood bedtime stories—like a dream come true.

Amin hurried over to Hilda, apologising. "I'm sorry to leave you alone. I wanted to make sure Nyla and the baby were safe."

"As you should," she replied with a faint smile. She had no intention of becoming a burden.

Meanwhile, the station manager spotted Hilda and, noting her Western appearance, walked toward her and Amin with cautious curiosity. Perhaps he thought her presence would reflect well on his station. With calculated steps, he approached Amin, sizing him up—would he be friendly, or distant, as a privileged foreigner? Amin's black suit, blue tie, and slightly rumpled shirt, along with the European-style hat he held, suggested a sophisticated background.

"Welcome to Baghdad, Doctor," the manager said, bending slightly as if offering a regal greeting. Though Amin had returned without the doctorate he had hoped to earn, he accepted the greeting politely. He noticed the station inspector whispering details about the passengers to the manager, recounting tales overheard during the journey. Amin felt a pang of anxiety; his association with Hilda might draw suspicion in this city divided between German sympathisers and British loyalists. Officially, Iraq was in a state of war with Germany, being under British mandate, and European Jews had sought refuge in various parts of the Middle East. He worried the British authorities might suspect him, Nyla, or Hilda of German sympathies. Yet the new Iraqi government was eager for independence from Britain and expressed sympathy toward Germany, making Baghdad a hub for espionage, suspicion lingering over all.

As they reached the main gate, Hilda drifted away from her companions, wandering into the busy streets in awe. She had expected to see the birthplace of Sinbad, Ali Baba, and the tales of *Arabian Nights* she'd read in her childhood.

She was snapped from her reverie by a gentle tap on her shoulder and turned to see a woman, her plump figure draped in a long abaya. The woman lifted the abaya's veil, revealing an olive-skinned face with kohl-lined eyes and lips painted in dark red lipstick that barely matched her warm complexion.

"Do you need any help?" the woman asked in Arabic. Though Hilda didn't understand the language, she caught the woman's meaning and answered in broken English, "I want to go to the station."

The woman, excited to encounter a foreigner, responded in English, "I'm Eva, a schoolteacher. I studied in the USA." Hilda was both surprised and relieved but remained cautious, wary of strangers. "Are you a Polish soldier?" Eva asked. "I've seen some women soldiers here in Baghdad—they're fighting to liberate their country from the Germans."

She wondered which side of the fence the woman was on. Was she with the British, making Hilda her enemy? Or was she against them, perhaps sympathetic to the Germans? Deciding it was safest to keep her guessing, Hilda pretended not to understand the language. Sensing Hilda's unease, Eva accompanied her back to the station's main gate and handed her a card. "This is my school's phone number. Please call if you need anything."

Just then, Nyla dashed over, visibly shaken. "Where have you been? We were worried!"

Hilda hurried to the waiting taxi, an old British Anglia. Inside, the car rocked and vibrated over the bumpy road. Amin took the opportunity to explain Iraq's recent history, from the struggle among European powers for control over its oil and strategic position to its symbolic importance in the region. Hilda listened, absorbed in the unfamiliar yet welcoming atmosphere around her, momentarily forgetting her own sorrows and worries. For a moment, she felt a deep connection to this corner of the earth. She wondered if it was the warmth and acceptance of the locals, especially her adopted family, Nyla and Amin, or perhaps some historic tie linking her to this place.

The taxi jolted suddenly, sending Hilda and Nyla forward against the seats. The driver struggled to open his window, finally lowering it to shout at the driver of a horse-drawn wagon whose confused horses had blocked the road. The trio burst into laughter at the scene, while baby Harb cried out in protest.

"Welcome to the East," Nyla whispered in Hilda's ear, grinning.

Chapter Fourteen

Settling Down in New Surroundings

Days in Baghdad flew by too fast. Hilda had moved into Amin's parents' home—a house built about a decade ago in a modern Western style, situated on the outskirts of old Baghdad. The area, Al-Adamyia, had gradually transformed from a small village, once known for supplying Baghdad with fresh fruits and vegetables from its proximity to the Tigris River, into a posh suburb. Affluent Baghdadis were moving here for the spacious, Western-style homes.

Amin's family had made their wealth from agricultural land in western Iraq and high-paying government jobs to help build modern Iraq. His father had risen to become a prominent minister in the newly established government, enjoying all the perks and privileges that came with such a position. Originally from western Iraq, the family had moved to Baghdad, where they had pursued higher education—something uncommon for most Iraqis since the days of Ottoman rule. Under British rule, the British had preferred to govern with the help of an educated workforce, creating a constitutional monarchy with a king from Hejaz (now Saudi Arabia) as a reward for his loyalty against the Ottomans. They established a parliament to represent the diverse factions of the young nation, modelling it on the British system.

As they arrived, a middle-aged gardener in a traditional white dishdasha hurried over to greet Amin and the others. He kissed Amin's hand and avoided direct eye contact with the women, greeting the group warmly while focusing on the men. He seemed intrigued by Hilda, the foreign woman in their company, but would wait expectantly for the maids to fill him in, anticipating the story would spread quickly among the neighbours. The gardener, with the driver's help, carried their luggage inside.

An elderly woman appeared in the doorway, adjusting her white scarf to cover her hair as she hurried toward them. Ignoring everyone else, she grabbed baby Harb, from his mother's arms, exclaiming, "My grandson!" Tears filled her eyes as Amin pulled her into a hug, momentarily quieting the baby's cries. "We're here, Mother," he said reassuringly.

"I was so afraid I'd never see you again!" she replied, still clinging to him, barely noticing the other women watching with a mixture of curiosity and sympathy, like an audience to a live Greek tragedy.

Nyla stepped forward. "How are you, Aunty?"

Amin's mother gave her a quick, perfunctory kiss on each cheek. "I'm fine, my dear. Do we have guests?" She turned to Hilda, giving her a shy look as she scanned her from head to toe.

"She's Hilda, our friend. She's been looking after Harb," Amin explained, his words landing uncomfortably on his mother, who struggled to hide her disapproval.

Hilda nodded politely in greeting, though she sensed the reserved response was slightly inadequate in this new cultural context where warmer welcomes and physical gestures were the norm.

Amin's mother led them through the small garden, with blossoming orange trees perfuming the fresh air and the calming sound of water trickling slowly from a nearby stream to water the plants. Amin took the chance to move closer to his mother, who seized the opportunity to whisper urgently, "Who is she? Does she speak English? Is she English or German?"

"She's German," he whispered back softly.

"Be careful, my dear. Is she a spy?" she murmured so low he could barely hear her.

"No, Mother. She was persecuted and fled her country. She's a German Jew."

The revelation left his mother momentarily speechless.

"Don't worry, Mother. She's safe, but we need to keep this quiet from the servants and everyone else for now."
"What will we tell our neighbours?"
"We don't have close neighbours—just farms, Mother."
"I mean family and friends."
"Tell them she's Harb's governess."
His mother sighed. "I wonder what your father would have said if he were alive." Her tone hinted at her doubts.

"He would have said, 'Help a desperate person in need,'" Amin replied, moving toward the entrance of the house. Built in a mix of Art Deco and Belle Époque styles, the home featured a grand entrance leading to the spacious living room and guest room. He opened the door to his father's office, which adjoined the living room, to explain to his mother the grim situation in Europe, and Germany in particular. His mother was ahead of her time, having completed primary school—a rare feat for girls of her generation. She hadn't been thrilled that Amin married Nyla, even though she was a relative, as she had hoped he'd choose a more educated partner.

Finally, the elderly woman rose, with some difficulty, and announced loudly, "She is one of our family." Her approval was crucial to Hilda's survival.

Chapter Fifteen

How to Become a Baghdadi!

The days passed, and summer was at the door. By mid-July, the heat was immense. Days began early and ended with a brief afternoon siesta, resuming again after sunset as people and businesses filled the streets with noise and bustle, announcing the night. The luckiest among the middle class could enjoy a fan to create a refreshing breeze, while most sought relief in well-insulated homes made of brick and mud or found shade under trees or in cool cellars of old Baghdad houses. The wealthiest even had newly introduced American-style water coolers.

Hilda found the headscarf and heavy clothing increasingly stifling, covering nearly her entire body to appear as a "decent woman" by local standards. Indoors, she noticed many Baghdadi women wore Western clothes, yet outside they adhered to social expectations by covering their bare arms and cleavage. Amin's mother had advised her, "A stranger must behave." The message was clear: "When in Rome, do as the Romans do." Hilda understood and accepted the warning.

While waiting in the lounge with the other women of Amin's family, Hilda learned that the Jewish seamstress was due to arrive to measure the ladies for new dresses. The goal was to update her wardrobe in line with local customs. Hilda was intrigued to share this experience. She knew from her father that Jews originally came from the Middle East. So while in Baghdad, she hoped to explore the rich Jewish heritage of the city and country, dating back millennia and contributing to its culture.

The maid entered and whispered to Amin's mother, "Kurchia has arrived". Hilda noticed the excited expressions of the women, both older and younger, as they prepared to greet her. The younger women aimed to impress potential suitors with their elegance, while the older women wanted to display a refined style associated with social standing. Each woman hoped to receive Kurchia's best design, and their greetings gave her a regal entrance. Kurchia, a woman in her late thirties, was bare-headed, wearing a white dress adorned with red flowers, high heels, and a luxurious leather handbag. Her olive skin was accentuated with makeup that highlighted a Roman nose and gazelle-like eyes, making her age hard to estimate.

Amin's mother, eager to reinforce her own high status, welcomed Kurchia, saying, "We have a guest from abroad." Hilda felt herself the centre of attention, Amin's mother proudly showing her off. The presence of a Western woman mingling with local ladies was a novelty, as Baghdadis generally referred to any Westerner as "The English," regardless of nationality. The British had ruled the country since World War I, so the locals were more accustomed to seeing British officials than other Europeans.

The other women, dressed in elegant strapless chiffon dresses tailored by Kurchia, appeared of a higher social echelon than the seamstress, yet Kurchia was no less sophisticated. She admired the women's dresses as her own creations, flattering one young woman in pink, "The dress fits your slender figure beautifully" although a hint of worry crossed her face as she considered the woman's thin frame. Her compliment petted the woman's ego, although mothers tended to prefer their sons' brides to be plumper.

Hilda, seated quietly, observed the women's behaviour, noting how Nyla took the initiative as hostess despite her mother-in-law's discomfort. Nyla's better English and German skills gave her a sense of superiority, so she translated the endless questions and fielded the ladies' curiosity about this foreign woman among them. Hilda was particularly intrigued by Kurchia, on learning from Nyla that she is a Jewish woman from Baghdad.

Turning to Kurchia, Hilda asked in broken English, "Where do you live?" Kurchia, responding in fluent English, explained that she lived in the Jewish quarter of central Baghdad, Kanbar Ali. Proud of her heritage, she eagerly shared details about the rich Jewish history of the city, noting, "Babylon was mentioned in the Talmud, you know." Hilda was unfamiliar with this religious context, having neglected religious studies, but Kurchia continued with pride in her knowledge. Nyla, relieved to stop translating, smiled as Kurchia went on, recounting Jewish history in Mesopotamia since the Babylonian King Nebuchadnezzar II exiled the Jews to Babylon.

"Can I visit that part of the city?" Hilda's question thrilled Kurchia, who eagerly offered to guide her through the historic buildings of Kanbar Ali. Hilda felt the need to reconnect with her ancestral culture, perhaps influenced by her near-death experiences and desire to understand why her people were often met with hostility.

Whether God existed or not, Hilda thought, "there's comfort in holding onto a belief in times like these." She knew, however, not to discuss her religious background openly.

Kurchia's wit and business acumen distinguished her as a modern, liberal woman. She suspected Hilda might be one of the many European Jews seeking refuge, and sensing Hilda's hesitation, she added warmly, "You're welcome to visit. I live with my mother and sister since my husband passed. I have no children," she finished with a hint of sadness. The other ladies shared sympathetic looks before Kurchia continued, more cheerfully, "My mother is an amazing cook, and I'd be happy to make you a nice dress." She eyed Hilda's dated outfit with a discerning look.

Hilda looked to Amin's mother for approval, who responded with a hint of authority, "There's no harm in refreshing your wardrobe, Hilda."

The maid entered, balancing a tray of tea as she struggled to walk on the freshly waxed Italian marble floor. She shuffled her way toward her mistress, carefully avoiding the faux statues of Sumerian goddesses scattered throughout the living room.

"Madam, the food is ready." The old lady dismissed the maid with a faint wave, as if she didn't exist. "Ladies, let's have something to eat."

The women stood up and followed the old lady to the dining room like soldiers behind their officer. They took seats at a large dining table that could accommodate twice the number of guests present. Hilda wasn't sure if dining this way—the Western style—was common among the less affluent families in Baghdad. She noticed the embarrassment, or perhaps the uncertainty, on the ladies' faces, revealed through their gestures and expressions as they attempted to observe Western etiquette in her presence.

The others waited for the German lady to sit and begin eating so they could follow. Hilda realised that this formal dining style might be reserved for special occasions and that, at home, their meals were likely much more informal. Hilda had previously dined with Amin and his family, seated at tables with the barest amount of cutlery. Sometimes, they ate using only spoons or, on rare occasions, seated on the floor. The women looked at her attentively, awaiting her signal. She hesitated before whispering in broken Arabic, "Let's eat." Nyla smiled, sensing that Hilda's casual manner subtly challenged her mother-in-law, who now seemed pleased to follow Hilda's lead.

Amin had confirmed with both Hilda and Nyla that Hilda's background should remain private, with only the fact that she was a German woman joining her husband, who worked across the Middle East, being shared. Amin and Nyla had befriended her and her husband in Berlin. For the sake of etiquette, the ladies refrained from discussing politics or religion. Still, they couldn't avoid brief comments about the waning British power in the region and its effects on the pro-British Iraqi government and the monarchy. Some Iraqi politicians were beginning to look toward Germany, hoping its rise could help counter British influence and support Iraqi independence.

The language barrier kept Hilda from revealing much about her personal life to the curious middle-class women, though she couldn't escape the local gossip surrounding an "English" woman living with Amin's family.

The table was loaded with Baghdadi dishes: vine leaves and other vegetables stuffed with rice, spiced minced meat, and herbs, known as *dolmas*. There were also trays of *kuba,* a dish made of cracked wheat filled with minced meat, alongside okra in a rich tomato sauce served with rice topped with vermicelli and toasted nuts. Despite initial aversion, Hilda grew to love the Baghdadi cuisine. She missed German sausages, which were hard to find in Iraq, though Nyla once prepared *basterma,* a spiced, garlicky sausage made by the Christian communities in the north. Later, desserts were served—fruit and a sweet rice pudding flavoured with saffron.

The women returned to the sofas after the meal. A maid entered with a tray bearing a pot of strong black tea, pouring it into small glasses and offering sugar generously—a rare treat, as Hilda learned that sugar rationing had begun due to the war, with resources redirected for British needs. Out of courtesy, she asked for just a small spoonful. The maid returned with another tray of citrus fruits and apricots. Nyla whispered, "You'll have to wait until summer for a wider variety."

"I'm grateful for what's here," Hilda replied modestly. "In Germany, oranges are only for Christmas." Her remark surprised the other women. Kurchia, more worldly due to her profession and her interactions with Europeans, leaned in and asked in broken English and Arabic, "Don't you have fruit in Germany?"

Sensing Hilda's embarrassment, Kurchia was quick to add, "I didn't mean to pry," though Hilda kindly replied, "We have apples and strawberries in summer." Nyla stepped in to interpret, though Kurchia's proud look suggested she understood perfectly well.

The women exchanged glances, whispering in Arabic as they assessed the simplicity of European food compared to their own. Middle Eastern cuisine, with its variety and sophisticated recipes, was evidently held in higher regard. Kurchia then boldly suggested, "Why don't we take Hilda on a tour of Baghdad?"

Nyla's mother-in-law looked horrified, hoping her guest would believe that all Baghdadis lived as she did. As part of her generation, she believed women belonged at home, attending to their families. Hilda, however, was eager to explore the lives of the working class, knowing that middle-class families like Amin's were rare.

Nyla raised a faint cheer, "Yes, let's go to Kanbar Ali; I haven't been in years."

"I know it like the back of my hand. I grew up in the Jewish quarter," Kurchia murmured with pride.

Kurchia and Nyla exchanged smiles. "Let's do it," they said in unison, while Amin's mother looked at them with a mixture of puzzlement and disapproval. To Nyla, this outing felt like a small taste of freedom.

Chapter Sixteen

Tourist in Baghdad

The news on the streets had grown grimmer. The war in Europe raged on, with Hitler's forces successfully invading more and more European countries. Preparations were already underway to extend German influence into North Africa, making rapid access to the Middle East seem like only a matter of time. The Jewish community in Baghdad had caught whispers of the atrocities suffered by European Jews under Nazi occupation, but the information came with limited detail. Meanwhile, the newly elected Iraqi government appeared to flirt with the Nazis, hoping to rid the country of British dominance and gain full independence based on Hitler's promises. The masses, already resentful of British influence, viewed the Zionist plans to establish a Jewish state in Mandate Palestine with even greater animosity.

Despite the war and food rationing, the Baghdadis refused to let these concerns dampen their daily routines or fun loving spirits.

Hilda had mastered Arabic impressively fast, much to everyone's surprise. Nyla and Amin often corrected her grammar, sometimes joking about her accent or her unusual sentence structures, particularly her struggles with plural forms. "You're learning Arabic as fast as my son Harb!" Nyla laughed, a comment that drew disapproving looks from her mother-in-law, who considered such loud laughter unseemly for a respectable lady.

"I'm sure Harb will master it before I do," Hilda responded, matching Nyla's humour with a hearty laugh of her own. Amin's mother frowned, puzzled and uncomfortable with the young women's animated behaviour, which she found improper.

A maid suddenly burst into the room, her face anxious. "Phone call for you, ma'am," she announced. The three women exchanged curious looks, wondering who it could be. Amin's mother, as the family matriarch since her husband's untimely death, stepped in to clarify. "Who is it for?" she asked with authority.

The maid's dark eyes scanned the room, finally landing on Hilda. "It's for you, ma'am," she said. Hilda, unsure she had understood the maid's accent, turned to Nyla for help.

Nyla took charge. "I'll get it," she said, standing up. Her slim figure in a red chiffon dress caught Hilda's attention, the dress revealing a bit of cleavage. Nyla left the room, making her way to the large, black telephone on a marble-topped table by the entrance.

Hilda and Amin's mother exchanged an uncomfortable glance. Hilda couldn't shake the feeling that she was not entirely welcome in the older woman's eyes. Moments later, Nyla returned with a wide grin. "Guess who called?" she asked, her voice lively.

"How would I know?" Hilda replied, genuinely puzzled.

"It was Kurchia!" Nyla exclaimed, despite her mother-in-law's clear irritation. "She's invited us over for dinner."

"That's rather short notice," Hilda remarked.

"Ha! People just drop by here without warning," Nyla laughed. "Consider it a courtesy that she even called."

Nyla turned to Hilda, her eyes sparkling with amusement. "Welcome to the East."

Amin's mother opened her mouth to say something, but Nyla quickly addressed Hilda. "Let's get ready. I adore the way Baghdadi Jews prepare food, and Kurchia's place always has the best atmosphere." She grabbed Hilda's hand, gently leading her out of the living room before her mother-in-law could issue any complaints.

Nyla whispered in Hilda's ear, "She's tough but kind-hearted. And we should ask Kurchia to sew a few dresses for you. She's the seamstress to the Iraqi royal family."

Hilda didn't fully appreciate the significance of this, but Nyla beamed with excitement. Nyla then instructed the maid on caring for her baby, quickly breastfeeding him before retreating to her room to change. She re-emerged in a floral dress that hugged her curves, briefly admiring her reflection in the mirror. "Pregnancy hasn't ruined my body," she muttered, donning a black abaya to cover the dress before her mother-in-law could scold her for immodesty.

Hilda put on a conservative black dress that covered her arms and chest. "Do I need to wear an abaya too?" she asked.

"No need," Nyla assured her. "You're well covered. Besides, you're a Western woman, so it's fine. Most Jewish and Christian women here don't wear abayas."

The gardener hailed a taxi for the two ladies. The driver, polite and respectful, kept his gaze lowered as they drove down Al-Rashid Street, one of Baghdad's newer, more modern areas built in the early 1900s. Hilda's eyes widened at the sight of a grand department store.

"That's the Orosdi-Back," Nyla explained proudly. "The first department store in Iraq. We must come shopping sometime and have tea or coffee afterward."

Hilda marvelled at this Western-style establishment in a relatively young nation. Noticing her surprise, Nyla elaborated, "It's a French company, modelled after the Wertheim department store in Berlin."

Hilda's thoughts drifted to her past, recalling the glamorous yet competitive job market in Berlin, and how the Nazi government had expelled the Jewish owner in 1933, forcing her to find work elsewhere.

The car weaved through narrow streets, barely wide enough for a single vehicle, as people strolled down the middle of the road and carriages pulled by donkeys ambled alongside them. Before long, they reached the Kanber Ali district, where the pungent smell of open sewage hit Hilda's nostrils, in stark contrast to her host's more affluent life. The scene reminded her of the bomb-ravaged parts of Berlin, yet there was a vibrancy here that kept her mesmerised. The air was filled with the loud, animated calls of street vendors enticing passers-by to buy their goods, mingled with the constant din of shoppers bargaining to lower prices.

The market stalls were simple yet resourceful, covered with makeshift canopies of old fabric supported by wooden poles, shielding both sellers and wares from the relentless sun more often than the brief winter rains. Local, seasonal fruits lay beautifully displayed, with more vegetables arriving as spring approached. Along the back of the road stood a row of humble shops: a butcher, a watch repairer, and textile vendors. Women draped in flowing abayas clustered around the fabric stalls, deep in spirited discussions, both amongst themselves and with the sellers, debating the perfect match of textiles and accessories for their dresses. A Jewish shopkeeper, with a well-practised charm, flattered the women's figures, assuring them that any of his wares would suit them—deliberately ignoring any physical imperfections that might suggest otherwise.

Their taxi struggled through the narrow streets lined with bustling market stalls. Eventually, the driver admitted defeat. "I'm sorry, ma'am, but we can't go any further," he said, embarrassed.

Hilda eagerly stepped out, wanting to experience the lively, chaotic atmosphere first hand. Nyla followed, taking instructions from the driver but soon getting lost in the maze of shouting vendors and donkey carts. Locals, used to seeing uncovered Jewish and Christian women but intrigued by the presence of a Western visitor, offered to guide them to Kurchia's house.

The house was an old Baghdadi residence, squeezed between two others. Its weathered facade hinted at stories of bygone eras. Kurchia appeared on the rooftop, dressed in a revealing outfit, and enthusiastically welcomed them. She hurried down to greet Hilda with four kisses on the cheeks, a gesture that made Hilda step back in surprise, unused to such intimate greetings from strangers. Growing up in Berlin's Jewish quarter, she had known warm embraces, but nothing so intense.

Kurchia led them through a wooden door into a passageway that opened onto a large courtyard dominated by a tall date palm beside a water well. Rooms surrounded the courtyard, and curious female relatives peered at Hilda as if she were an alien. Embarrassed, Kurchia shooed them away.

"Most of these people are family," Kurchia explained apologetically, her voice tinged with embarrassment. "Our house isn't as nice as Nyla's."

"I find it fascinating," Hilda said warmly, boosting Kurchia's confidence.

"What would you like to drink?" Kurchia asked, addressing Hilda with excitement.

A teenage girl rushed down the stairs, and soon a tray appeared, piled with date- and nut-stuffed pastries, alongside a large pot of black tea. The tea was served in small, transparent cups, with sugar settled at the bottom. Kurchia, eager to impress, asked, "Do you take milk in your tea? We don't here."

"No, I'm German," Hilda replied. "We prefer coffee and never drink milk with our tea, like the English."

Kurchia looked a bit disappointed, but Hilda added, "Nyla has introduced me to the local tea, and I love it."

"She's practically an Iraqi!" Nyla laughed, and the others joined in, their laughter covering any embarrassment.

The meeting was supposed to be a social visit, but they planned to return for dress measurements. "I'll revolutionise your wardrobe," Kurchia declared confidently. Nyla frowned, discomfort flashing across her face. But Kurchia's attention remained on Hilda, whose indifference to fashion seemed to puzzle her.

Nyla stood up. "Thank you, Kurchia, but we should be heading home."

"Please stay! I'm making lamb and rice. It's halal, not kosher, by the way," Kurchia said.

While Nyla tried to assert herself, Hilda stepped in, attempting to mediate. "I understand. Halal is quite similar to kosher. We observe it at home."

The mention of "kosher" made Kurchia's eyes light up with recognition, while Nyla tensed, worried about the consequences of revealing Hilda's Jewish identity. Taking a chance, Kurchia whispered to Hilda, "You're Jewish, aren't you?"

Hilda, taken aback, nodded proudly. "Yes, I am."

Nyla entered the room and immediately sensed a shift in the atmosphere. Suspicion and uncertainty hung thick in the air. The three ladies exchanged glances, their eyes drifting uneasily to the damp stains on the ceiling.

Chapter Seventeen

Life Goes On

Summer was approaching quickly, and with it came the relentless rise in temperature. Hilda felt it more acutely than the others. The heat seemed to intensify by the day, if not by the hour. Her tolerance for such high temperatures was low, but she made an effort to get used to the climate, albeit with some difficulty. She had taken to sleeping on the flat roof of the house, where she enjoyed watching the stars in the clear night sky and felt some relief from the electric fan during the day. Although the fan's loud hum was hard to ignore, she knew it was a luxury not afforded to many. Most of Baghdad's lower-income residents had no access to electricity, and the maid explained how they wet their clothes for some fleeting coolness or use nets of dried, spiky desert plants called "Akol," sprayed with water, or try to catch a draft in the open courtyards of their homes. The fortunate ones in bygone days even had servants to fan them.

Life in Baghdad truly came alive after sunset. Families gathered in gardens or courtyards and often took evening strolls along the Tigris River to catch a breeze. Nyla, meanwhile, was reconnecting with her social circle after years away in Europe and the responsibilities of raising a young child. She resumed visits with relatives, old schoolmates, and neighbours, eagerly sharing stories of her time abroad. The Baghdadi women were fascinated by her tales of European life and even more intrigued to meet Hilda, whose Arabic had improved remarkably. Hilda's every action—from her manner of dress to her eating habits—was observed with a mix of admiration and critique.

News travelled fast in Baghdad, even with limited communication channels like radio and newspapers, which often echoed political sentiments. Hilda heard from Amin about the horrors unfolding in Germany, particularly the atrocities against the Jews. Despite her discomfort and the burden she felt she placed on her hosts, she was grateful to be far from that nightmare. Yet thoughts of her son haunted her. She feared she had lost him, either to the war or the Holocaust, and struggled to bury these worries. The British propaganda machine was unrelenting, emphasising the dangers of Nazi Germany and reinforcing the stability of the British-backed local government.

The newly elected Iraqi government, led by Prime Minister Rashid Ali Al-Gaylani, was pushing for independence from British rule and warming up to Nazi Germany, exploiting nationalist sentiments. The accidental death of King Ghazi, who had openly opposed British influence, had only fuelled anti-British sentiment.

"I'm worried about Hilda," Amin whispered to Nyla in their bedroom.

"Why? She's a harmless woman," Nyla replied, her voice soft and innocent.

"If the Iraqi government aligns itself with the Germans," Amin continued, "Hilda, as a German Jew, could be in serious trouble. Remember, her presence here is technically illegal. She entered without proper documents and can't approach the German embassy, since we're at war with them. Hostility towards the Iraqi Jewish community, who have lived here for thousands of years, is rising. Hilda is no exception."

"You're scaring me," Nyla said, her voice now tinged with worry.

"I'm scared too," Amin admitted. "My mother is pressuring me to ask Hilda to leave."

"We can't do that," Nyla insisted.

"I know. I don't have the heart to tell her, but we might need to find another arrangement," Amin said, his face flushed with guilt over his selfish concern. "If the government punishes us, I could lose my postgraduate study funding or worse."

"What should we do?" Nyla asked, now more concerned for their family than for Hilda.

"For now, we need to keep a low profile," Amin advised. "Please don't take Hilda out. Let's make sure she stays under the radar."

Nyla's gaze shifted to the window, where the roses in the garden were scorched by the golden rays of the sun. She let out a heavy sigh, knowing that summer would be long and winter far too short.

Amin gently whispered, not wanting to wake the baby, "Try to sleep, darling. Maybe things will be clearer tomorrow."

"Good night," Nyla whispered back, her voice even softer, as she wondered what the future held for them all.

Chapter Eighteen

Spring Terror, 1941

The short snap of winter had passed, making way for a fleeting spring. Hilda basked in the sunny days, finding particular joy in the blossoms that briefly decorated the vast garden. Yet, she knew the relentless summer heat would soon return. It astonished her to realise that more than a year had passed since her arrival in Iraq. Restricted by what felt like a semi-house arrest, her walks were now confined to the greenery around Amin's home, and though she missed her long wilderness strolls, she was grateful for the sense of safety Amin and Nyla provided. Life felt like an open prison, but she resolved to balance her gratitude with her responsibility to maintain a low profile.

Despite the challenges, Hilda often reflected on the warmth and generosity of the locals, which far outweighed the negative aspects of her situation. She filled her days with discipline, almost like a Prussian soldier, diving into Amin's vast collection of history books. She found immense pleasure in learning about Mesopotamian history and even assisted Amin with editing his thesis, correcting grammatical errors and refining his prose. The three of them—Hilda, Nyla, and Amin—had become a close trio, managing a semblance of joy despite the ominous news from war-torn Europe and the rumblings of political tension in Iraq.

One of Hilda's favourite memories was visiting the marvellous arches of the ancient city of Ctesiphon, the former capital of the Persian Sassanid Empire. Locals referred to the ruins as "Taq Kasra," the majestic archway that had survived centuries. As spring flowers adorned the site, families gathered to enjoy picnics before the oppressive summer heat took over.

The family planned a similar outing to Taq Kasra.

"You'll need to wear this black abaya and hide your European looks," Nyla said with a playful laugh, handing Hilda the heavy, silky garment.

"Necessity is the mother of invention," Hilda teased back, struggling to wrap herself in the slippery fabric. The three of them, joined by friends, drove to the outskirts of Baghdad in Amin's old Helmin car, eager to soak in the beautiful spring day.

Hilda attempted to mingle with the crowd but was always wary of revealing too much about herself. She remained unsure whether to disclose that she was German, Jewish, or keep silent altogether. Feeling restless and yearning for adventure, she eventually whispered to Nyla, "I'd like to walk to where the Diyala and Tigris rivers meet."

Nyla's face clouded with anxiety. "It's dangerous. What if you get recognised or lost?"

A family friend, who had helped secure Hilda's papers, reassured Nyla with a nod.

"I'm looking after my son right now," Nyla said, hesitant. "But I'll ask Amin to escort you."

"Oh no, please don't disturb him," Hilda insisted. "I can find my way."

Nyla reluctantly agreed, and Hilda wandered off, marvelling at the grape farms and towering palm trees. The mild spring sun soon reddened her fair skin, and her abaya struggled to stay in place against the breeze. For a fleeting moment, she relished her newfound, albeit temporary, freedom. Her thoughts drifted to Germany, her childhood, and the son she had left behind. Was he still alive? Guilt overwhelmed her as she wondered whether she had betrayed him by fleeing to safety.

Lost in her musings, she suddenly realised she had strayed far from familiar sights. Panic crept in, reminding her of the terror she felt fleeing the Gestapo. Desperately scanning the field, she saw no sign of human activity. Tears threatened to spill when a voice shouted in the distance. She turned to see a black dot on the horizon, slowly transforming into a young woman carrying a bundle of firewood on her head. The woman's sun-bronzed skin and confident stride suggested a life spent outdoors.

Fear guided Hilda's instincts, and she rushed toward the girl, who dropped her bundle in surprise and hailed her in Arabic. After several awkward exchanges and attempts at communication, the two women began to understand each other using gestures. The young woman introduced herself as Sabria, and Hilda reluctantly agreed to follow her through the field, grateful for a lifeline. As the sun dipped into the horizon, painting the sky orange, they walked in shared silence, each comforted by the other's presence.

Sabria led Hilda to a small, tight-knit village of mud-brick houses, where the novelty of a foreign woman's appearance caused a stir. Children surrounded her, wide-eyed with curiosity, and women peeked from behind headscarves, while men scrambled to offer assistance. A young man with a thick moustache approached, speaking halting English. "Can we help you?" he asked, his words a balm to Hilda's frayed nerves.

He ushered her into a small living room, simple but cozy, with rugs covering the floor and cushions arranged around a central space. The men respectfully stepped out, leaving Sabria and the interpreter. Hilda was offered watered-down yogurt, which she reluctantly sipped, not wanting to offend her hosts. Meanwhile, the men began slaughtering a sheep to prepare a feast, and the women busied themselves with cooking.

Hilda watched, overwhelmed by the hospitality. Soon, a meal of tender meat, vegetable stew, and fragrant rice was served on a large tray. Though she wasn't hungry, she accepted the food to show her gratitude. The villagers waited for her to eat first, then joined in, savouring every bite. A cup of strong, sugary black tea followed, soothing her and aiding digestion.

As darkness fell, Hilda grew anxious. The women prepared a small, bare room for her to sleep in, offering her a mat, a blanket, and a kerosene lamp. They left her with warm smiles and reassurances, though one young girl stationed herself at the door, ready to serve Hilda if needed. Exhausted, Hilda lay down, her thoughts returning to her son, her homeland, and her adopted family in Baghdad. She felt like she had betrayed Amin and Nyla, but the worry lulled her into a restless sleep.

At dawn, a sudden knock and shouts jolted her awake. Women wailed and called her name, and she hurriedly grabbed her abaya. The village elder took charge, issuing orders. Outside, a British Anglia police car waited, and two young officers approached. One, who spoke passable English, informed her, "Your family is very worried."

The word "family" struck Hilda deeply. It wasn't her family in Germany but Amin and Nyla who had become her true loved ones. The policemen led her to the car, and Hilda waved goodbye to the villagers who had shown her such kindness. As the car sped down the unpaved road, dust obscured everything behind her, but she smiled, thinking, *I'm not alone in this world.* Yet, she couldn't help but wonder, *Will I always have to leave things behind?*

Chapter Nineteen

In the Midst of Political Turbulence

Amin and Nyla kept a watchful eye on Hilda's movements since her recent misadventure. Though she felt slightly suffocated by their extra care and protection, Hilda had come to accept it as part of her reality. After her journey to the countryside, the couple began questioning her whereabouts more frequently. Hilda missed the joy of mingling with the Jewish community in Baghdad, which had been facilitated by Kurchia. The times she spent at her house or the local synagogue fulfilled her spiritual needs and provided some comfort for the emotional void created by her forced departure from her homeland. Her near-death experience had only deepened her religious connections.

The world's political situation continued to escalate, reflecting the raging war in Europe. Alliances shifted rapidly, with nations constantly recalculating their positions based on battlefield gains and losses. The Germans were making significant advances in Europe and North Africa, emboldening some Iraqi politicians and military leaders who hoped for liberation from British control. Iraq, under a British mandate, was heavily influenced by the British Embassy, which acted as the country's ruling authority. The Nazi German leadership had started appealing to Arab nationalism, promising independence and self-rule. This rhetoric resonated with the increasing nationalist fervour in Iraq.

Rashid Ali al-Gaylani, the recently elected Prime Minister, sought greater independence from the British, and his government leaned toward the Germans, believing they might help Iraq break free from British influence. The streets of Baghdad buzzed with talk of independence and the possibility of prosperity from oil wealth. Yet, while oil revenue began to flow, most of it went to international corporations or corrupt officials, leaving little for the masses.

Hilda walked through Amin's family garden in the Wazireya district, enjoying the brief feeling of liberation. An old maid recounted the family's history and how they moved from their old home in Karagol, near Medan in central Baghdad. Hilda was surprised by the maid's knowledge. Wazireya was named after an Ottoman governor, or *wazir*, and the district featured modern houses with expansive gardens. The early spring breeze hinted at warmer days ahead.

"Shall I make you a coffee?" the maid asked in a soft voice, her black scarf tied as a sign of her age and adherence to cultural norms.

"Yes, please," Hilda replied. She had developed a fondness for Turkish coffee and Iraqi cuisine, although she noted that her waistline had expanded from the family's indulgent three-course meals.

Nyla appeared at the garden's main gate, returning from a shopping trip to Rashid Street with her friends. Hilda had wished to join her but remained at home, following Amin's mother's orders to maintain a low profile.

"Hilda shouldn't be seen in public too often," the matriarch had declared.

Hilda approached a flower bed, inhaling the roses' fragrance. The weather was growing warmer, although the maid insisted it was still mild for this time of year.

While Hilda smelled the roses, Nyla's soft voice interrupted her reverie. "Hello, Hilda. Sorry you missed the shopping. It was wonderful." Nyla handed a few shopping bags to the maid, who silently hurried inside.

"I thought it best to keep a low profile after getting lost and with the tense political atmosphere," Hilda replied, though she inwardly disagreed with being secluded from society.

"I'm sorry you're caught in this mess. At Orosdi-Back, I could hear everyone talking about the government changes and recent events," Nyla said, her tiny face showing signs of worry.

She added, "You remember the shopping centre we visited once?" Nyla seemed eager to remind Hilda that Baghdad had its own sophistication, comparable to Berlin.

"What happened?" Hilda asked, steering the conversation to the point, ignoring Nyla's attempt at reassurance.

"There's been a military coup," Nyla explained, her voice dropping. "The royal family is under house arrest at the palace. The crown prince, Abd al-Ilah, has fled the country, scared for his life."

Hilda's worry deepened. "What if a pro-German government takes over? Should I flee Iraq? I don't want to put you in danger," she said, her voice tinged with despair.

"Don't worry," Nyla reassured her. "Amin has a safety plan. You just need to stay out of sight and not leave the house without us."

"Do I have a choice?" Hilda whispered to herself.

She gazed at the horizon. The roses in the flower bed were starting to yellow, despite the mild early spring heat—a reflection of the shifting and uncertain political climate. Hilda wondered just how far she would have to run from her homeland to feel truly safe.

Chapter Twenty

An Uncertain Departure

Fast cars raced away from Zuhur Palace, the royal residence situated near the Washash River on the outskirts of Baghdad. The palace, built in the 1930s and designed by British engineer Gibson, had a modest yet elegant structure, and housed the newly established royal family since 1921. On this fresh April morning, a convoy of Rolls-Royce and Austin cars moved slowly across the tarmac, carrying the teenage King Faisal II and his mother, Queen Aliya, to an undisclosed destination. Rumours on the streets hinted that they were being taken to a place of forced residence.

The political atmosphere had been simmering since winter, following the appointment of Rashid Ali Al-Gaylani's government. Opinions about this administration varied: some described it as pro-Nazi, others as merely anti-British. Public beliefs were divided, with many harbouring a grudging sympathy for the young king, who had lost his father, King Ghazi, in a suspicious car accident. Speculation ran wild that British embassy officials or the pro-British former Prime Minister, Nuri Al-Said—who had also fled the country in fear—were somehow involved.

In Iraq, news was carried more by word of mouth than by official media. Hilda trusted the saying, *"No secrets in the East,"* and found rumours to be more reliable than the heavily censored reports from newspapers and radio stations, which were often aligned with political factions. Her anxiety had grown to the point that she rarely left her room, only venturing out for meals at Nyla's gentle insistence. Even then, Nyla's mother-in-law would make no effort to hide her discontent, disliking the presence of an outsider in their home—a foreigner with a complicated background, whom her son and daughter-in-law had apparently become very attached to.

Hilda had often overheard the older woman speaking to her son, Amin, in Arabic, understanding enough to pick up on the concerns expressed. The family worried that Hilda's German-Jewish heritage put them at risk. To the pro-British faction, she was an enemy for being German, while to the pro-German faction, her Jewish identity marked her as a potential threat. There seemed no way for Hilda to escape her predicament.

Hilda woke early that morning but remained in bed, feeling listless and devoid of hope. She felt like a hostage, despite the kindness of her hosts. A knock at the door interrupted her thoughts. Before she could respond, Nyla entered, her expression a mixture of worry and cheer.

"You're still in bed? Come on, wake up and join us for breakfast downstairs," Nyla urged.

"Sorry, I have no appetite," Hilda replied in a flat, tired voice.

"We're planning a trip to Al-Rashdiya, by the Tigris River. It's beautiful out there." Nyla's eyes lit up with pride.

"Your country is wonderfully beautiful," Hilda responded, her voice softening. "But I think I'd better stay here. I don't want to put you at risk. If you want me to leave, just say so."

A shadow of pain crossed Nyla's face. "I hope you understand our position. It's complicated, but we care for you deeply. Even Harb is attached to you." Tears welled up as she embraced Hilda.

"I would never bring harm to anyone," Hilda whispered.

Nyla's heartfelt words weren't enough to change Hilda's mind. When the rest of the household left for their picnic, Hilda remained behind, her resolve firm. As silence settled over the house, broken only by the occasional sound of the gardener who had taken the opportunity to visit his own family, Hilda packed a small suitcase with essential clothing and toiletries. She wandered to Amin's study, her heart heavy, and sat at his mahogany desk. With trembling hands, she wrote a note in German:

Dear Amin and Nyla,

I cannot thank you enough for your hospitality and, more importantly, for saving my life. While my life may mean little to some, it has meant everything to you. I cannot continue to be a burden on your family. Please do not worry about me. I will be safe. Somehow, I feel it—I feel safer here than in my homeland.

Yours,
With love, Hilda

She left the letter open on Amin's desk, then rushed to the main entrance. Her suitcase contained only a few dresses, two pairs of shoes, and scarves. Clad in an abaya to blend in and hide her striking features, she checked her handbag for the few Iraqi dinars she had saved. The money came from German lessons she had given to local academics hoping to study in Germany after the war.

Taking a deep breath, Hilda stepped outside, passing through the small front garden. She looked up at the house that had become a temporary sanctuary and whispered, "Will I ever return?"

She walked toward the main street, careful to budget her limited funds. Approaching a long Ford bus, she asked the driver in her carefully rehearsed Arabic, "Do you go to Akad Al-Yahood?"

The driver nodded in astonishment. He knew the Jewish quarter well. A young man offered her his seat, and she handed two fils to the driver's assistant, who kissed the money in gratitude. The old bus weaved through the tranquil streets of Wazireya, heading toward the bustling heart of Baghdad. Hilda thought of Kurchia's earlier offer to host her should she ever become too much of a burden on Amin's family.

"It can't be any worse," she murmured to herself, watching as life bustled on, oblivious to her silent turmoil.

Chapter Twenty-One

New Place, New People

The sun shone fiercely, stronger than usual for late May, marking the end of spring and the beginning of a long, scorching summer. The bus driver's assistant called out loudly, "Kamber Ali!" His voice was husky, and his manner exuded a forced bravado, as if he took pride in acting as a protector for the Western woman before him. It was a rare sight to see a white, Western woman using public transportation typically reserved for the working class. He made a point of stopping the vehicle, stepping out to guide Hilda through the maze of narrow alleys, and called over another young man to assist her.

"She's a foreigner," he whispered to his companion, who respectfully avoided making eye contact with Hilda and led the way ahead of her, not in keeping with the Western norms she was accustomed to.

Kamber Ali was shaded by buildings so closely packed that they blocked out direct sunlight, providing a welcome respite from the heat. The district was a labyrinth, designed like other old cities to confuse invaders—a necessity given Baghdad's long history of conquests. Hilda felt a brief sense of relief in the cooling breeze that passed between the houses and down the narrow streets. The area was familiar but disorienting, and she struggled to find the exact address.

Her guide finally stopped in front of a wooden door, intricately carved with Arabic designs. He knocked with surprising force for someone of his small frame. A young maid, appearing startled, answered the door. The guide quickly introduced Hilda, mentioning the name "Kurchia," which the maid seemed to recognise. She stepped aside, allowing Hilda into a house she had visited only a few times.

Voices speaking Judeo-Arabic drifted down from the upper floors. Hilda sat by a small fountain in the courtyard, hoping the feeble trickle of water would provide some cooling relief. A voice interrupted her thoughts.

"You can't go wrong sitting by the shatherwan," Kurchia said, approaching. She wore a light, floral gown that accentuated her curves and revealed a bit of cleavage. Despite being in her mid-forties, Kurchia's skin glowed, well-preserved against the harsh Baghdadi sun.

"It's lovely here," Hilda replied, fanning herself with a palm-leaf fan she had picked up from a nearby table. "I don't know how you cope with the heat."

Kurchia smiled, her voice authoritative yet warm. "You wait for the real heat to come. It'll be one of the hottest summers yet, having started so early this year."

"How do you know that?" Hilda asked, using her Western logic.

"The elders say so. Their long experience is our best guide," Kurchia replied confidently.

Hilda's eyes drifted to the blue tiles lining the fountain. "I don't see any newspapers around," she noted.

"We don't read much," Kurchia responded hesitantly, her words suggesting she wasn't entirely truthful.

"Well, bad news travels fast, as the English say," Hilda murmured in English, finding it easier to express herself that way.

"You know, your Arabic has improved," Kurchia remarked, perhaps to change the subject or genuinely impressed.

Hilda managed a faint smile. "Thanks to Amin's mother and the maid. I practised with them a lot. Amin speaks German fluently, Nyla somewhat less so, but her English is as good as yours."

Kurchia beamed at the compliment. A compliment from a German woman, who are known for speaking their minds, felt particularly flattering. Hilda's thoughts wandered to her abrupt departure from Amin and Nyla's home—the family who had saved her from the horrors of Europe's Holocaust. Memories of her son and her homeland weighed heavily on her mind.

A loud knock interrupted her reverie. She was relieved that, unlike local Muslim women, she didn't have to cover her hair. Kurchia, however, asked the maid to fetch a white cotton cardigan to cover her bare shoulders. Hilda pitied her in the heat.

The maid opened the front door, and Hilda recognised the familiar male voice exchanging greetings in Arabic. It was Amin, dressed in a black suit and tie, attire that seemed entirely impractical in such sweltering weather. Hilda stood as he approached, breaking cultural norms by hugging her. Tears welled up in her eyes, while Amin tried to maintain a stoic demeanour.

"Why did you leave? he asked, his voice firm. "Did someone upset you?"

"I didn't want to bring any harm to you," Hilda replied, avoiding his gaze. "How did you know I'd left?"

"We couldn't continue our picnic. The streets became unsafe, and the army blocked the roads. We had to come back. Nyla was in tears when the gardener told us you had gone."

"How did you know I was here?"

"Where else would you go but to Kurchia?" he replied.

Kurchia, observing the emotional scene, reassured Amin. "Don't worry. She's safe here. The Jewish community is well respected in this country, and we can protect her. Hilda's Arabic is good enough for her to pass as a Kurd, Armenian, or Christian Assyrian. She'd be far more exposed at your house, where prominent politicians and dignitaries visit regularly."

Amin looked down, feeling he had failed to protect Hilda. "Nyla and my son miss you."

Hilda's heart ached. "Send them my love and kisses. I hope we'll see each other once this turmoil passes."

Kurchia offered Amin a drink, but he declined politely and left hurriedly. As he disappeared out the door, Kurchia turned to Hilda and sighed. "He's a good man."

Hilda nodded. "Indeed. He and his wife are my saviours. Now it's your turn to keep me safe."

"Mind you, his mother is quite difficult," Kurchia noted, curious if Hilda shared the sentiment.

Hilda only smiled and said, "She's a mother who would do anything to protect her children, like any mother would".

Kurchia, who had chosen to remain unmarried to care for her family, took the statement to heart. Their eyes met, and she pulled Hilda into a warm embrace.

Chapter Twenty-Two

Before the Storm

The temperature climbed relentlessly, as if mirroring the escalating political unrest in Baghdad. By late May, the heat was palpable not only in the air but also in the charged atmosphere of the city. A military coup had overthrown the British-backed government, ushering in an administration with known ties to the German Nazi Party. This new alliance inflamed nationalist sentiments, as well as a dangerous wave of anti-Semitism that quickly spread from Europe to Iraq.

German propaganda, amplified through radio broadcasts and media, struck a sensitive chord by focusing on Jewish immigration to British-mandated Palestine. The Jewish community in Baghdad was on high alert. For thousands of years the Jewish community in Baghdad had enjoyed a peaceful coexistence with their Muslim and Christian neighbours, contributing significantly to the city's economy and culture through their expertise in fine arts, trade, and jewellery craftsmanship, enhancing the allure of a metropolis that had once been the capital of a great empire. However, the fragile harmony of centuries now stood on the brink of collapse.

A meeting was convened at a local synagogue, bringing together Jewish leaders and influential Muslim and Christian figures. The atmosphere was tense, as concerns about the safety of Baghdad's Jewish community hung heavily over the gathering.

"I have lived in this city for decades without ever feeling as estranged as I do now," an elderly Jewish man said, adjusting his kippah and dabbing at his sweat-drenched forehead.

"This unrest is temporary," the hakham reassured, stroking his long white beard. "I have seen tensions rise and fall many times over the years. This, too, shall pass."

"We have always lived in peace with people of other religions in this tolerant city," a Christian leader added, glancing toward the Muslim clergy for affirmation.

The Muslim cleric, adjusting his kufi, scanned the anxious faces in the room. While his outward demeanour remained calm, he struggled to mask his own fears. "Yes, harmony has been the foundation of our shared history," he said. "It is outside propaganda that sows discord among us, serving only foreign interests."

The Christian priest stood, his posture commanding as if delivering a Sunday sermon. "The situation is complex. The streets are simmering with anger over the events in Palestine. The clashes between Zionist militias and the Palestinian uprising dominate the news. That anger could easily spill into our own neighbourhoods."

All eyes turned to the hakham, who flushed with embarrassment or perhaps fear. His voice trembled but grew steady as he spoke. "The Jews of Baghdad have been here for thousands of years. We have lived together in peace and mutual respect. We have no connection to Zionist actions in Palestine."

Several attendees nodded in agreement, some patting his shoulder in reassurance. But the tension in the room was palpable.

The hakham continued, his tone resolute. "We must trust in the goodwill of the majority to ensure the safety of our community. However, we also need a plan to safeguard our lives and livelihoods."

The Christian priest sighed heavily. "Let us hope this does not lead to violence and destruction."

Attention shifted back to the Muslim cleric, who now felt the weight of leadership in a predominantly Muslim society. He knew that many in the public viewed the Palestinian struggle as a religious conflict, a misconception that could spiral out of control.

"I will do my best to calm the situation," he said cautiously. "But we cannot ignore that the current government aligns itself with Nazi

Germany in exchange for promises of independence from British rule. They may do anything to appease Hitler."

"I will do my best to ensure our community is not swayed by the current anti-Jewish propaganda. However, let us not forget that Iraq has many Christian sects, and some still hold the belief that the Jews handed Jesus over to the Romans."

This statement did not go down well, leaving the Jewish dignitaries visibly shaken. A low murmur of voices grew into a louder hum as the tension mounted, saying. "Not true."

"It's a historical claim that has never been proven," the Jewish priest replied defensively, facing the Christian clergyman's puzzled gaze.

The attention shifted back to the Muslim clergy, who hesitated to make a promise he knew he might not be able to keep. He felt like a mouse cornered by a predatory cat.

"I will do my best to ease the situation. However, let us not forget that our current government is a strong ally of the German Nazi regime, lured by promises of freedom from British control. They will go to great lengths to appease Hitler."

The words struck like thunder, especially among the Jewish dignitaries. As the meeting ended, the attendees exchanged looks of fear and uncertainty. Outside, the relentless sun beat down, and the streets of Baghdad seemed poised for a storm that no one could yet predict.

Chapter Twenty-Three

Another War

The old radio blared martial music from its spot on the wooden coffee table in Kurchia's courtyard. The announcer's voice, filled with enthusiasm, anger, and anxiety, added to the charged atmosphere. Hilda, already consumed by unease, felt the music pierce through her like a storm. She wanted to shout, hit, and kick but felt reduced to the role of a helpless bystander, scared and small.

Political turmoil had reached its peak. The April 1941 military coup, the house arrest of the pro-British royal family, and the growing influence of the German Nazi-backed regime under Prime Minister Rashid Ali al-Gaylani had thrown the city into chaos. The alliance between the pro-Nazi Golden Square officers and German forces only intensified anti-Semitic sentiment, leaving the Jewish community on edge.

Kurchia and her family sat transfixed by the radio, ignoring even the soothing melodies of their beloved Jewish singer, Salima Murad. Hilda gauged the severity of the situation as Kurchia's attention remained fixed on the unfolding news.

The tension was contagious. Hilda, sipping tea and nibbling on date-stuffed klecha, tried to feign indifference, but her memories of war came flooding back in vivid flashbacks. Her fragile truce with the past was shattered. Though Kurchia had sheltered her from much of the outside world's turmoil, it was now impossible to shield Hilda completely.

Having picked up a fair grasp of Baghdadi Arabic and the local Jewish dialect, Hilda overheard whispers and commentary that deepened her unease. On one occasion she was mistaken for someone from Mosul during while chatting in the marketplace.

All of a sudden a frantic knock at her door startled her. "Please come down quickly," Kurchia's trembling voice called out, barely forming the words. Without hesitation, Hilda grabbed a long black robe to cover her see-through nightgown and hurried downstairs, sweating in the oppressive heat.

Soon, the deafening roar of planes overhead was followed by the sound of bombs. The fragile walls of the old house trembled, and glass shattered across the floor.

"They've done it! The Abu Naji British have come to our rescue!" Kurchia's elderly uncle proclaimed, using the local nickname for their British occupiers, which implied a begrudging respect.

"They might rescue us, but they could also kill us!" Kurchia retorted sharply.

"If the Germans had taken full control, they would have exterminated the Jews in Iraq, just as they're doing in Germany. Ask your friend," the uncle said, glaring at Hilda with barely concealed hostility.

Hilda, ever the outsider, bore the brunt of his scorn. To most of the Jewish community, she was an anomaly—her appearance, culture, and experiences set her apart. She was "English" to them, a term applied to anyone with a Western or European demeanour, regardless of their actual nationality.

The alienation weighed heavily on her. *I belong nowhere,* she thought bitterly. *Not German in Germany, yet German here. Jewish in Germany, but not here.*

Her inner turmoil mirrored the heated arguments unfolding around her. Fear and confusion filled the air as family members debated who was to blame for the chaos, though none truly had a hand in its making.

The bombing intensified, shaking the city and its people to their core. Religious elders began reciting verses from the Torah, seeking solace in their faith as explosions rattled the walls. British military planes targeted key government and military installations, including the Ministry of Defence near the Tigris River.

After days of relentless bombing, the Iraqi forces loyal to the prime minister were overwhelmed by British military might. The radio announcer, his voice dripping with triumph, declared the restoration of the pro-British Prince Abd al-Ilah, who had returned from refuge in Iran. The prime minister fled to Germany, while the leaders of the Golden Square coup were publicly hanged at the gates of the Ministry of Defence.

The influx of news and political analysis left Hilda reeling. The polarised opinions reminded her painfully of Germany in the 1930s.

The atmosphere grew increasingly tense. Hilda felt trapped, unable to leave the house, and burdened by the nagging sense that she was an inconvenience to her hostess. Despite Kurchia's reassurances that she was safe and welcome, Hilda couldn't ignore the occasional uneasy glances directed her way.

Hilda couldn't dismiss the nagging question in her mind: *How much of this is real, and how much is my own paranoia?*

Chapter Twenty-Four

A Knock at the Door

The heat of early June pressed heavily on the first day of the month. Kurchia knocked on Hilda's door, urging her to come down for breakfast. Hilda, lacking any appetite, hesitated but remembered the local custom—declining food was akin to refusing friendship. Suppressing her straightforward German instincts, she forced herself to join the family, hoping to mend any unspoken rift caused by recent events.

She sat at the table, sipping sweet black tea, its heat burning her lips. Kurchia served freshly baked naan, white sheep cheese, and fried eggs cooked in fragrant *dehan hur*—concentrated butter. The aroma momentarily lifted Hilda's spirits as she tore a piece of bread to dip into the golden yolk.

A sudden, forceful knock shattered the fragile calm. Startled, Hilda spilled her tea onto the floor. Kurchia rushed to the door, her voice trembling.

"Who is it? What do you want?" she called out, her body unsteady.

"They're coming! Beware!" shouted a panicked, unfamiliar voice.

"Who are you?" Kurchia demanded, but no response came. Instead, gunshots echoed through the air, followed by terrified screams.

Hilda moved toward Kurchia, but her hostess quickly pushed her back.

"Go inside!" Kurchia whispered urgently, her voice low, trying to protect her guest from whoever was outside.

The two women exchanged frightened glances, frozen in shock. Gradually, other members of Kurchia's family came down, their faces pale with fear. Some had been upstairs while others had gone to work or the market.

Kurchia's elderly uncle, trying to muster courage as the head of the family, stepped forward. His frail body, powered by a surge of adrenaline, ignored Kurchia's protests as he unlatched the door.

"Oh no!" he cried, recoiling as he saw a dead man lying crumpled on the doorstep.

"We need to hide—quickly!" he stammered.

Panic spread as everyone scrambled for cover. Some squeezed beneath the sofas, while Hilda sought refuge in the small, cramped toilet. The muffled shouts of an approaching mob grew louder. Then came a deafening crash as the door was broken down, and the angry crowd poured into the house.

Hilda, trembling, struggled to secure the toilet door. She could hear furniture being overturned and people screaming. Moments later, the door burst open, revealing a middle-aged man with a thick moustache and dark skin. He was wearing a traditional *dishdasha* and holding a dagger aimed directly at her.

Panic-stricken, Hilda reverted to her mother tongue, blurting out in German, "I am German!"

To her astonishment, the man paused. He quickly hid the dagger behind his back and spoke to her in halting English. "You... German?"

Before she could respond, his accomplices entered, one of them pointing a gun at her. Hilda's heart sank. She braced for the end, flashes of her son's face racing through her mind. A strange calm washed over her as she thought, *Maybe I'll see him again in another world.*

Sitting on the cramped toilet, she closed her eyes, awaiting her fate.

"She's fine! She's not Jewish—leave her alone!" one of the men barked in Arabic.

The man with the moustache gave a respectful nod and motioned for the others to leave her be.

Hilda exhaled sharply as they retreated, leaving her alone in the suffocating silence. The noise of the mob gradually faded, replaced by the deafening roar of her thoughts.

What am I going to do now? she wondered, her mind spiralling in a storm of fear and uncertainty.

Chapter Twenty-Five

Life after Farhud

The oppressive heat of early June mirrored the simmering tensions in Baghdad, where the aftermath of the Farhud pogrom had left a city struggling to regain its footing. The once-bustling streets began to show signs of life again, but a palpable sense of unease lingered in the air. People cautiously resumed their routines, visiting reopened shops to purchase food and clothing after days of chaos. Yet, the atmosphere was heavy with mistrust and fear, especially among the Jewish community, whose centuries-old bonds with their neighbours had been shattered almost overnight.

In the Jewish quarter, the streets were quieter than usual. Small groups gathered around vegetable stalls, their conversations hushed and filled with uncertainty. Shops bore the scars of violence, their windows shattered, and their shelves emptied. Jewellery stores, once glittering with wealth, now stood gutted, their treasures stolen by the mob.

The word *Farhud*, meaning "violent dispossession" in Arabic, had become ingrained in the vernacular, spoken in hushed tones among the city's residents. The synagogue in the heart of the Jewish quarter became a gathering place for the bereaved, where families awaited the burial of loved ones. The traditional rituals of washing and praying over the dead were rushed and incomplete, as safety concerns and the sheer number of victims overwhelmed the community.

Couples of policemen loitered nearby, their indifference stark against the grief surrounding them. Smoking foreign cigarettes, such as Camel, Lucky Strike and Old Gold, obtained as bribes, they offered little reassurance to the mourning families. They were meant to provide protection in case of any further reprisals.

Kurchia, cloaked in a black *abaya*, stood among the mourners. Tears streamed down her face as she mourned the loss of her uncle, a casualty of the riots. Rumours about his death varied: some painted him as a hero who had defended his family, while others suggested his frail heart had simply given out amidst the chaos. Regardless of the cause, his loss weighed heavily on Kurchia and her family, who saw the tragedy as a test of faith.

From a distance, an old black Austin car came to a halt, unable to navigate the narrow alleys. A veiled woman emerged, her blonde hair barely concealed beneath the black fabric. She approached the funeral cortege cautiously before making her way toward Kurchia.

"I'm truly sorry for your loss," she said, her voice trembling.

On recognising the voice, Kurchia turned to face her, her expression a mix of sorrow and anger. "Thank you," she replied curtly, making it clear that Hilda's presence was unwelcome.

"I had nothing to do with this," Hilda began, her German bluntness pushing her to defend herself.

Kurchia's eyes blazed with anger. "My uncle would still be alive if he hadn't come to your rescue."

Hilda's voice cracked as tears welled up. "I was hiding in the toilet when the mob found me. They were German sympathisers, and I told them I was German, not Jewish. They took me away, thinking I was a hostage. Your uncle tried to intervene, but his heart couldn't take it. I never meant for this to happen."

"So, he's dead, and you're alive," Kurchia spat. "You didn't even have the courage to admit you're Jewish, hiding behind your German identity. My uncle gave his life for someone who wouldn't claim her own people."

Kurchia turned her back on Hilda, signalling the end of their conversation. She walked away, shielding her family from the woman she now saw as a harbinger of misfortune.

Hilda turned away, her steps heavy with the weight of shame as she retreated from the crowd. The men gazed at her foreign beauty with curiosity, while the women whispered bitter words of disdain. Hilda climbed back into the car and ordered the driver to take her far away, anywhere but here.

The events replayed in her mind as the car rolled through the streets. The mob had initially planned to take her to the German consulate, an act that could have sealed her fate. The consulate was a hollow presence, with no real authority left after the riots. She had managed to escape the mob's grip by blending into the chaos, donning a black scarf looted from a shop to disguise her identity as a Westerner, aware that she could be targeted as German, British, or Jewish, depending on the political leanings of those around her.

Hilda's thoughts turned to the affluent Waziriyah suburb, where the Sassoon family lived, near Amin's mother house. They were a wealthy, affluent, and influential family, with prominent members who contributed significantly to finance and politics in shaping modern Iraq. Hilda had visited them before with Kurchia and Nyla and hoped they might offer her refuge. They had welcomed Hilda intermittently, either as a German or a Jew, depending on the shifting political climate, having maintained a good relationship with the British authorities over the years.

Nevertheless, alliances to power often shift. The British authorities heavily relied on the Jewish community during the establishment of modern Iraq, valuing their skills, education, and the adoption of a policy that granted minorities limited political and financial power to counterbalance the impoverished majority.

However, the British began distancing themselves from the Jewish community due to recent unrest in Palestine and Baghdad. Hilda was compelled to prove she had been persecuted by the Nazi regime, seeking validation from her old friends Nyla and Amin to gain access to the Jewish elite. She felt that the Jewish community's centuries-long contributions to the development of Mesopotamia had been undone in mere days.

When she arrived, the family welcomed her cautiously. The family was exploring the possibility of relocating to another country, either temporarily or permanently, depending on the circumstances. They offered her a room but requested that she keep a low profile while they assessed their options. At dinner, the head of the family, Heskael, sighed heavily. "I cannot leave my country," he said, his voice resolute.

"We have no future here, Grandfather," his grandson countered, ready to abandon his life of privilege for the unknown.

Hilda sipped her lentil soup in silence, avoiding the gazes of those around her. The focus of their conversation weighed heavily on her.

"What is the next step?" she wondered. "Where do I go from here?"

Chapter Twenty-Six

Bound for Bombay

A cortege of British-made cars queued outside the 1930s-built mansion in the Wazireya suburb of Baghdad, preparing to depart in haste. Two maids and the driver loaded large suitcases into the cars while an elegant elderly lady gave orders from inside. The rest of the household rushed around her like bees following their queen, unquestioningly obeying her commands, rational or not.

Mrs. Samha Sassoon, the family matriarch, was a formidable figure whose authority was rarely challenged. Her two sons darted through the house, collecting precious ornaments, following her directives without hesitation. Even her husband, the head of the family, deferred to her. In a society where men outwardly exuded machismo, the true power often lay with the women, their influence hidden beneath abayas.

Samha entered the room briskly, her expression betraying her anxiety. "I'm not sure this is the right move," she hissed, her words failing to mask her fear.

"We have no choice," her husband replied in a calm, measured tone, trying to reassure her. "We don't feel safe here anymore after the recent events."

"But things have calmed down now," she countered confidently. "The King has returned, and the pro-British government is back in power."

Her husband acknowledged her knowledge of Iraqi politics, gained from years of befriending politicians' wives and members of the royal family. Still, he shook his head gravely.

"That may be true, but we won't receive any support because we're Jews. The streets are turning against us. Nazi propaganda has poisoned minds, and events in Palestine have only made things worse. The British no longer favour us, not after the Zionist militias' actions against their troops in Palestine."

"What does that have to do with us?" she exclaimed, her voice tinged with disappointment. "We've been here for thousands of years, living peacefully alongside every sect and religion."

"Sometimes, hysteria blinds people," he said, bitterness lacing his tone. "They forget the past, their friends, even their families. Eventually, the frenzy subsides—people have short memories. But for now, we need to disappear, at least until the dust settles."

"British India is our safest bet," he explained. "We have extended family in Bombay—Jews who settled there centuries ago and prospered as merchants. With the capital we have, we can build a decent life. This move is for the boys' future."

"India? What will we do there?" she asked, her frustration mounting.

Samha sighed deeply. "I'm still unsure."

"I've made arrangements," he assured her. "I've paid bribes and secured support from certain politicians. We'll carry enough cash to sustain us. But as a Jewish member of parliament, I've been increasingly alienated. My role is no longer tenable."

"What about her?" Samha snapped suddenly, her tone sharp with jealousy.

"Who?" he asked, feigning ignorance.

"Hilda," she said pointedly. "Your favourite. It's not that I don't like her, it's just she is a liability."

"She's a poor Jewish refugee," he replied. "We're in the same position now. It's our duty to help her—our Torah teaches us that saving one life is like saving the whole world."

Samha couldn't argue against the Torah. With a resigned tone, she said, "Very well, she can accompany us as the boys' teacher."

Her husband sighed, relieved by her compromise. Though deeply devoted to his wife, he couldn't help recalling his youthful infatuation with a German girl during his time at the Iraqi consulate in Berlin. Hilda's presence stirred faint echoes of those memories, but he kept such thoughts to himself.

A light knock on the door interrupted them.

"Come in," he called, his voice firm.

Hilda entered, her steps small and timid. She wore a light blue chiffon dress embroidered with gilded flowers, a gift from a wealthy Jewish woman. Her golden hair gleamed in the soft light, perfectly complementing the dress. Mr. Sassoon's gaze lingered on her, though he quickly masked his admiration.

"Please, sit down," he said, gesturing toward a chair.

Hilda obeyed, her posture modest yet graceful. "I'm so grateful for your kindness during these difficult times," she said, her voice filled with emotion.

Mr. Sassoon leaned forward. "We're planning to leave Baghdad temporarily, until the situation stabilises," he began.

The news sent a chill through her. *Where will I go if they leave?* she thought, panic welling inside.

"We are planning to go to India. You're welcome to join us," he continued in a paternal tone, "but the choice is yours. If you have other options, we'll respect your decision."

Samha interjected coolly, "It's not an easy move for us, and we can barely save ourselves from this mess. But you're welcome to come—if you wish." Her words were polite, but her tone betrayed a hope that Hilda might decline.

Hilda hesitated, lowering her gaze. "Where else can I go if not with you?" she murmured, her voice trembling with uncertainty.

Chapter Twenty-Seven

Route to India

The train finally departed from Baghdad International Train Station after hours of delay. Hilda carried her suitcases with difficulty, trying to avoid the station porter who had rushed to assist her. She knew his help would come with the expectation of a tip, but she also felt the weight of cultural norms—seeing a white woman carry her own luggage was considered improper.

The journey from Baghdad to Basra was a relatively recent development, an achievement proudly attributed to British administration. This particular leg of the railway line was celebrated as a symbol of progress, but the heavy fumes from the locomotive, mingled with its deafening noise, left little room for romanticism.

Hilda sat beside Mr. Sassoon, who kept her close to create the impression that she was an Englishwoman. Her European appearance worked to the advantage of the fugitive Jewish family, helping them evade the scrutiny of Iraqi authorities. Yet, tension lingered in the air. Mrs. Sassoon's trembling hands betrayed her nervousness, even as she tried to maintain an air of composure. She glanced at her two sons, who sat across from her. Both were immaculately dressed in tailored black suits, their hair neatly styled to mimic the Hollywood actors they admired.

Mr. Sassoon, ever the politician, opted for a practical grey suit and a coordinated tie. While his wife concealed her figure beneath a flowing black abaya, her husband looked less polished than usual but retained his characteristic dignity. He sat with a quiet unease, his wife ensuring that he kept his distance from Hilda. When the train lurched forward suddenly, luggage tumbled down, startling the passengers. Hilda let out a faint gasp, but Mrs. Sassoon's loud cry drew concerned glances. She quickly silenced herself, acutely aware of the attention she might have attracted.

As the train continued southward, its stops became frequent and unpredictable. The compartment filled and emptied with each station. Noticing the discomfort caused by the overcrowded space, the train inspector approached Mr. Sassoon.

"Sir, there's an empty compartment available if you'd prefer more comfort," the inspector murmured, hoping for a tip.

Mrs. Sassoon seized the opportunity. Turning to Hilda, she said with forced politeness, "You should take it, dear. It'll give you a chance to rest." Her triumphant glance toward her husband made her intentions clear—she would not leave Hilda alone with him.

Hilda accepted the offer, and the older son, Albert, leapt to help her with her luggage, his enthusiasm unmissable.

"Albert! Where do you think you're going?" his mother called sharply, her tone betraying her annoyance.

"I'm helping Hilda, Mother," he replied, trying to sound nonchalant but failing to hide his eagerness.

"You'll return immediately. Let the inspector handle it," she snapped, deliberately using the Iraqi pronunciation of his name to emphasise her displeasure.

Hilda was shown to the compartment, a small, cold space that felt even chillier in the winter air. Though she welcomed the reprieve from the crowded main carriage, the biting cold was a stark contrast to the oppressive heat she had grown used to. Exhausted, she settled in for a nap, her dreams carrying her back to her homeland and the memories of her son.

She woke to the sound of soft footsteps outside the compartment. A faint knock followed, accompanied by a low male voice.

"Albert, what are you doing here?" she asked groggily, stifling a yawn.

"I came to check on you," he replied timidly, stepping into the room.

"I'm fine, but your mother will worry," she said, observing him carefully. He was a striking young man with olive skin, a neatly trimmed moustache, and a suit that fit him as perfectly as if he were a mannequin.

Albert hesitated before speaking, his voice thick with emotion. "Actually, I wanted to tell you something."

"What is it?" Hilda asked, her curiosity piqued.

"I love you," he confessed suddenly, the words hitting her like a thunderclap.

"Albert, I could be your mother," she replied, her voice a mix of regret and disbelief.

But something stirred within her. Since her husband's untimely death, Hilda had denied herself the possibility of intimacy. She had dedicated her life to raising her son and working as a schoolteacher, suppressing her own needs in the process.

Albert stepped closer, placing a strong hand on her shoulder. She felt the warmth of his touch and did not resist as he leaned in to kiss her. His attempts at passion were clumsy, reminiscent of a boy mimicking the suave heroes of Hollywood films. She reciprocated at first, then pulled away sharply when his fervour became too aggressive.

"Stop!" she cried, her voice firm.

"Why? Am I not good enough?" he asked, his disappointment palpable. "Even the prostitutes in Al-Medan said I was—" He stopped abruptly, realising too late how much he had revealed.

"It's not about that," Hilda said, adopting a maternal tone. "You're a young man with your whole life ahead of you. This isn't right."

"I want to be with you," he whispered.

Their conversation was interrupted by footsteps in the corridor. Albert stiffened, his face turning pale.

"It's probably my mother," he muttered. "I told her I was going to the toilet after escorting you."

He checked the hallway and, seeing it empty, left in a hurry.

Hilda sat alone, her emotions swirling. A part of her felt flattered, even awakened, by Albert's youthful desire. But another part was burdened by the impropriety of it all. "I can't afford such indulgences," she whispered to herself, pushing aside the pangs of loneliness and longing.

She knew she was not Mrs. Sassoon's favourite person, and this incident would only add fuel to the tension between them. Hilda felt trapped between her survival instincts and the stirrings of desires she had long suppressed.

Chapter Twenty-Eight

Tension on the Tracks

The train trudged slowly along the fertile Mesopotamian plains, flanked by the mighty Tigris and Euphrates rivers. The scenery was tranquil, with palm trees swaying gently and citrus groves dotting the landscape. The fields, kissed by the recent spring rains, gleamed in lush green hues, a testament to the region's reliance on irrigation and its agricultural bounty. This timeless land of wheat and water now served as the backdrop to the Sassoon family's uncertain journey.

Hilda was startled awake by a knock on her compartment door. The train attendant, a young Iraqi man with a distinct southern accent, greeted her. His dark olive skin and faint moustache contrasted with his eager demeanour. "Ma'am, Mr. Sassoon invites you to join the family for breakfast," he announced politely.

Still groggy from a restless night spent grappling with the intricacies of the Sassoon family dynamics—and the turmoil of Albert's earlier confession—Hilda thanked him in Arabic and rose to prepare herself. With no time to change clothes or freshen her appearance beyond washing her face at the rudimentary train lavatory, she glanced into the cracked mirror and muttered to herself, *"I still look good enough."*

Straightening her posture, Hilda strode down the narrow corridor, her confidence buoyed by a renewed awareness of her femininity. She knocked softly on the Sassoon family's compartment door and was met with a curt, commanding female voice: "Enter."

Inside, the family was seated around the small table. Mr. Sassoon greeted her warmly, standing as she entered. Albert's eyes lit up momentarily before he averted his gaze, a transparent attempt to hide his admiration. Meanwhile, Mrs. Sassoon's expression was icy, her painted face betraying the simmering suspicion beneath. Hilda, aware of the unspoken tension, sat cautiously at the edge of the seat, awaiting permission to engage.

Heskeal Sassoon—preferring Hilda to use his first name—smiled at her. "I hope you had a restful night, Hilda," he said, breaking the silence.

"It was fine, thank you, Mr. Sassoon," she replied, keeping her tone polite but restrained.

"Please, help yourself to breakfast," he said, gesturing toward the modest spread of boiled eggs, sheep cheese, bread, and steaming Iraqi tea.

Before Hilda could move, Mrs. Sassoon interjected in a cold tone, "Hilda isn't a stranger. She doesn't need an invitation." Her clipped words were accompanied by a barely perceptible sneer.

Despite the underlying tension, Hilda understood the cultural cue that guests should take the first bite. With deliberate hesitation, she reached for a slice of cheese and a piece of stale naan bread. "Please, dig in," Samha added, her tone softening slightly but her eyes still watchful.

Hilda sipped the sweet tea, appreciating its rich, fragrant warmth despite the knowledge of wartime shortages making such a luxury rare.

"Not to worry," Heskeal said, leaning forward with a knowing smile. "We'll have plenty of tea where we're headed." His cryptic comment suggested their intended destination while maintaining the pretence of a business trip to Kuwait.

As the train crossed a bridge, Heskeal reached out and lightly touched Hilda's shoulder, ignoring the sharp glare from his wife. "Look, Hilda," he said, his voice filled with pride. "The Mesopotamian Marshes. They're eternal—historic."

Hilda gazed at the sprawling marshes where the Tigris and Euphrates rivers converged, their waters merging into a vast expanse before flowing onward to the Persian Gulf. Tall reeds stood like sentinels above the water, their golden tips swaying gently in the breeze.

Birds of every colour and size flitted across the marsh, painting the landscape with vibrant life.

Albert seized the opportunity to impress her, his voice eager. "See those houses, Hilda? They're built entirely from reeds and float on the water. The Marsh Arabs have lived like this for thousands of years."

Hilda nodded, intrigued by the history and beauty of the scene, though her attention was interrupted by Samha's sharp glance at her son. Albert's brother, meanwhile, dozed in his seat, oblivious to the tension.

The train's inspector suddenly called out in a loud, firm voice, "The train will arrive in Basra soon!"

For a moment, the compartment's occupants exchanged furtive glances, united by the mutual apprehension of what awaited them at the next station. For now, the rhythm of the train and the uncertain road ahead bound them together, though cracks in their unity had already begun to show.

Chapter Twenty-Nine

An awakening in Basra

The train came to a sudden halt, accompanied by a piercing whistle that echoed through the station at Basra. Passengers instinctively plugged their ears with their fingers, trying to muffle the cacophony of the conductor's signals.

The train station, constructed by the British after they took control of Iraq from the Ottoman Turks during the First World War, bore the marks of practical military engineering. The rail line connecting Baghdad to Basra, initiated by the Germans before the war, was later completed by British forces. The rhythmic clatter of the steam locomotive was amplified by the bustling bazaar nearby, which had sprung up to cater to travellers with food, drinks, and clothing. As Hilda surveyed the scene, she noted, "Though smaller than Baghdad's station, it's just as noisy." But unlike many, Hilda found comfort in the chaos; the sounds reminded her of a Bach symphony, a blend of order and complexity. She had often listened to such music on Mr. Sassoon's gramophone while his wife enjoyed Salima Murad Pasha's melodic Jewish ballads.

As she stood at the platform, memories of *Arabian Nights* surfaced in her mind. She pictured the legendary Sinbad embarking on his daring voyages from Basra's port to the unknown. Her imagination brought the tales alive against the backdrop of this ancient city.

Porters rushed to carry the family's luggage, their movements quick and practised. A small, worn British Hillman car waited nearby, creaking under the weight of their belongings. Young Albert, eager to impress Hilda, was the first to tip the porter, stepping ahead of his father in a show of manhood.

The car wove its way through Basra's narrow streets, struggling to maintain balance. The fresh river breeze wafted in through the windows, mingling with the unpleasant fumes from the car's engine.

Hilda leaned forward to glimpse the vast waterway ahead: the Shatt al-Arab, where the Tigris and Euphrates rivers met before emptying into the Persian Gulf. The date palms lining the riverbanks swayed gently, their reflection shimmering in the waters below.

Mr. Sassoon, ever eager to play the historian, narrated the city's origins. "Basra was built by Arab Muslims around the 7th century AD as a military garrison to keep watch over the Sassanid Empire," he explained, struggling to translate the nuances of its history into English. Hilda nodded politely, more mesmerised by the picturesque surroundings than the lesson itself.

The car stopped at a modest three-story hotel. Its simple design carried an air of practicality rather than charm. The Sassoon family claimed the front room, overlooking a courtyard lush with palm trees and vibrant flowers thriving in the city's mild winter. Hilda's room was adjacent to the boys' room. The communal showers were basic but clean, with gender-separated facilities.

Hilda, eager to refresh herself after the long journey, was informed by the receptionist that hot water would only be available for three hours a day. Wasting no time, she hurried to the dimly lit bathroom, filled with the earthy, invigorating scent of olive-oil soap, which she savoured as it softened her skin and lifted her spirits. The scrubbing ritual reminded her of the luxurious communal bath experience she had shared with Nyla in Baghdad, complete with massage and pampering.

Wrapped in towels, Hilda hurried back to her room, her skin tingling from the brisk scrubbing. As she turned the corner, she was startled to see Albert waiting by her door.

"I've been waiting for you," he murmured, his voice carrying a mix of nervousness and desire.

"What are you doing here?" she asked, her voice unsteady, both fearful and uncertain.

"I miss you," he admitted.

Hilda froze. She was already walking a delicate line with Mrs. Sassoon, whose simmering jealousy was barely concealed. Hilda knew she was barely tolerated as it was, and that Samha would never forgive her if she lead her beloved son astray. A carefully arranged marriage with a young Jewish girl undoubtedly awaited Albert—a path where Hilda had no place.

Albert hesitated for a moment, then placed his hand on Hilda's bare shoulder. She felt a jolt at his touch. It had been years since anyone had touched her so intimately. Her resolve faltered as a long-dormant part of her awakened. In a sudden rush of fear, she pulled away and dashed into her room.

But Albert was relentless. He pushed the door open with firm determination, stepping inside and closing it behind him. "Albert, no!" she pleaded, her voice breaking in a mix of English, Arabic, and German.

He ignored her protests, his youthful passion overriding her resistance. But as the tension built, something shifted. Hilda, feeling the tenderness beneath his intensity, guided him with a gentle touch. The initial force of his approach gave way to a softer connection, as though both were learning to navigate an unfamiliar yet magnetic terrain.

For Hilda, the encounter stirred memories of her first love, her late husband, and the sweetness of youthful passion. What had begun as an act of recklessness transformed into a moment of mutual vulnerability, their whispered words replacing the earlier tension.

As the night enveloped them, Hilda lay awake, staring at the ceiling. A storm of emotions swirled within her—guilt, longing, and the ache of knowing this fleeting connection could lead to irreversible consequences. She knew the line she had crossed was dangerous, but for one brief moment, she had allowed herself to feel alive again.

Chapter Thirty

Under Watchful Eyes

The air was heavy with humidity from the sea breeze, making the city's oppressive heat somewhat more tolerable, though still difficult to breathe. Hilda had a light lunch at the hotel. Her host family had given her strict instructions: she was not to wander the city or set foot outside without their permission—more likely, without Samha's explicit consent. Confined to her modest hotel room, Hilda felt like a prisoner.

She scanned her surroundings: a wooden bed, a small mahogany wardrobe with two doors, and a tiny mirror. Approaching the mirror, she examined her reflection. Not too bad for a woman who had just passed her prime, she thought. She had never paid much attention to her looks—until her encounters with Albert. His youthful passion had stirred something dormant within her, something she thought had been lost long ago.

Albert's nightly visits had become a recurring affair, filling her with equal parts longing and dread. She feared his mother would eventually discover their liaison, jeopardising her standing with the family that had shown her such kindness. "Physical needs often take precedence," she whispered to herself in resignation, echoing a sentiment she'd observed in Middle Eastern culture.

A sudden, firm knock on the door jolted her from her daydream. She rushed to the mirror, hurriedly combing her hair and debating whether to apply makeup—a practice she was unaccustomed to. Anticipation quickened her heart. Perhaps it was Albert, stealing another precious moment away from his mother's watchful eyes.

Hilda eagerly opened the door, a soft, seductive voice slipping from her lips. "Who is it?"

"It's me, Samha."

The voice hit Hilda like an electric shock. Her excitement evaporated instantly.

Samha stood at the door, looking as if she'd just returned from a professional stylist. Her makeup was meticulously applied, masking years from her face, and her sky-blue dress revealed a cleavage of a woman that had passed her prime a long while ago. Hilda's unease was evident, and Samha seemed to mirror it. They had long mistrusted each other, Samha particularly resenting Hilda's influence over the men in her family.

"Hello, Samha. Nice to see you," Hilda greeted her with forced warmth, her voice trembling slightly.

"How are you doing?" Samha asked, though Hilda knew her well-being was the last of her concerns. Still, Hilda understood the Middle Eastern preference for indirect politeness, so unlike her own Germanic straightforwardness, which locals might easily mistake for rudeness.

"I'm fine, ma'am," Hilda replied, her tone subdued, like an obedient student addressing a strict headmistress.

Samha stepped inside, her expression shifting to one of measured severity. "I know you're direct, so I will try to be the same," she began. "You are welcome in our family as a gesture of loyalty to our people—the Jews."

Hilda nodded politely, waiting for her host to reach the point.

"My family is my most precious possession," Samha continued. "You could take my life, but not my family. I've worked tirelessly to keep us together through political and social turbulence, especially as Jews in this region. The rise of the Zionist movement and calls for a Jewish state have changed everything. My ancestors lived prosperous, peaceful lives here for centuries, but now... I'm not so sure about the future."

Hilda feigned attentiveness, her patience wearing thin.

"Let me be clear," Samha said, her tone sharpening. "Do not come too close to my husband or my sons. I know they're intrigued by you—your Western, European manner and your... reasonable beauty. To them, you're a novelty, something new and exciting. But men are like children. They play with a new toy until they tire of it and toss it aside. I don't want your relationship with Albert to become... too serious. You understand me, don't you?"

The words stung, but Hilda composed herself. "I can assure you, ma'am, that I have no malicious intentions toward your family," she said, though she felt humiliated. It was clear to her now just how much power the women in this household wielded, despite the outward appearance of male dominance.

Samha's stern expression softened, though her eyes remained watchful. "Good," she said. "We're going out tonight to the Port Club. It's a British establishment, and I worry about potential trouble if there are British members. They won't understand what it means to be a German Jew in these times."

"No problem," Hilda replied quickly. "I have a book to read here at the hotel. Please, take the boys with you."

Samha smirked, pleased by Hilda's reassurance. The message had been received.

"Certainly," she said, her voice laced with satisfaction. "I will."

Chapter Thirty-One

A Captain's Invitation

It was a hot June morning. Hilda stood on the deck of the commercial ship, gazing out at the endless horizon. She revelled in the challenge of breathing the hot, humid air, savouring the fleeting sense of freedom it gave her.

Mr. Sassoon had secured passage for his family and Hilda through a combination of favours, bribes, and his connections with the British Navy and commercial shipping authorities. The war had disrupted routine shipping schedules, but the British still prioritised military transport—moving personnel and munitions from India to Iraq and supporting efforts in Europe. Somehow, Mr. Sassoon managed to arrange an exceptional berth, a testament to his resourcefulness and past support for British interests in Iraq.

The ship glided smoothly over the calm waters of the Persian Gulf, eventually reaching the Arabian Sea without incident. The Sassoon family brought provisions for the journey—simple fare like cheese, bread, dates, and pulses for occasional cooking in the ship's galley. Mr. Sassoon also purchased British soldiers' rations, including tins of bully beef, much to Samha's disgust. She insisted they adhere to kosher dietary laws, preferring fresh lamb over the foreign canned goods and insisting that her husband give away the tin of Spam.

The sailors were courteous, but Hilda could feel their lingering gazes on her. She dismissed their timid glances as the harmless longing of men deprived of female company for months at sea. Still, she felt emboldened, choosing to wear more Western-style outfits despite Samha's disapproval. Samha, in a competitive spirit, tried to mimic Hilda's style, hoping to reignite her husband's interest. Her efforts earned her little more than pitying glances from desperate sailors, and when she fabricated tales of sailors making advances toward her, hoping to provoke her husband's jealousy, his only response was a curt, "Then cover yourself."

The ship's captain, a tall, middle-aged Scotsman named Fraser, had a commanding presence, softened by an air of melancholy. He had fought in the final years of the First World War and later married a German-Jewish woman he met in Belgium. She had died of tuberculosis, leaving him with a son now serving on the European front. Captain Fraser seemed to have a lot of sympathy for Hilda, whose plight reminded him of his late wife.

He insisted on inviting the Sassoon family and Hilda to dine with him in his cabin. Samha, though jealous, saw the invitation as a blessing—it redirected Hilda's attention away from her family. The captain, eager to impress Hilda, presented them with his finest French wine, a rare luxury.

The Sassoon family were delighted to accept an invitation from Captain Fraser. That evening, Hilda entered the captain's cabin like a figure out of Arabian Nights, followed by her entourage. She wore her only cocktail dress, a modest but alluring piece that accentuated her figure. Samha, not to be outdone, donned a similar dress sewn by Kurchia but was forced by her husband to cover herself with a cardigan, concealing her sagging arms and décolletage.

The captain exchanged lingering, lustful glances with Hilda, provoking Samha's jealousy. Meanwhile, the men in her family seethed with anger—not only at Hilda's daring choice of dress but also at the attention she was receiving from a man of authority.

The meal was of a simple European-style, consisting of boiled potatoes, beef stew, and tinned vegetables, prepared by the ship's inexperienced cook—a man who had taken the job to avoid fighting on the frontlines. He attempted to impress them by showing his culinary skills with a bread-and-butter pudding.

Conversation flowed in English, with Captain Fraser occasionally switching to German to impress Hilda. His attentions toward her were unmistakable, and the flirtation did not go unnoticed by the Sassoons. Albert, in particular, looked as if he might explode, his anger simmering just below the surface.

Sensing the tension, Samha intervened. "I do not mean to be rude," she said with a strained smile, "but we have the habit of going to bed early." She shot a warning glance at her family, daring them to object.

Hilda was about to follow suit, but the Captain stopped her. "I want to show you something, Hilda," he said.

Samha turned with a furious glare, realising she had lost control and that the power had shifted to Hilda. The Sassoons then left the communal area of the ship and retreated to their compartments. Hilda found herself sweating, unsure whether it was from the heat, the food, or the Captain's attentions.

She hesitated but responded with a faint, teasing smile. "What is it?"

"It's in my cabin," he said, his tone almost boyish.

He kissed her hand lightly and turned, walking toward the corridor. Hilda followed, one step behind, her heart pounding.

"Well," she thought to herself, "no one can say no to the captain."

Chapter Thirty-Two

En Route to a New Life

The morning was hotter and more humid than any Hilda had endured throughout the journey. Her breathing grew heavier, a stark contrast to the dry heat she had grown accustomed to in Baghdad. The difference was unmistakable as they sailed deeper into the Indian Ocean, far from the arid landscapes she once knew.

The sailors disrupted the early morning calm with shouts of excitement as the ship approached the shores. Their energy contrasted with Hilda's meticulous preparation. She packed her belongings with the efficiency and precision of a true German, ensuring nothing was left to chance. Meanwhile, the Sassoons argued in Arabic about how and who should handle their packing, Samha's commanding voice losing its edge amidst the chaos. Hilda chose not to interfere in their family matters but stood ready to offer assistance if Samha asked for it.

Hilda's position within the Sassoon family had evolved; she was no longer merely a guest but a figure who influenced their future, thanks to her association with Captain Fraser. Eager to catch her first glimpse of Bombay, she hurried to the deck, dressed in a light frock. The vast port came into view, dwarfed only by the horizon beyond it. She marvelled at its size compared to Basra's modest harbour. A question rose in her mind: *Is this freedom at last?*

Her thoughts were interrupted by a rough, calloused hand brushing against her bare arm—a hand that told a story of hard labour. She turned to see Captain Fraser leaning close, his broad shoulders casting a shadow over her. His lips hovered near her ear.

"You're beautiful," he whispered.

Hilda smiled, her expression signalling approval. Fraser began recounting Bombay's rich history, its vibrant culture, and its flourishing Bollywood film industry. She was fascinated. Memories of her late husband surfaced; they had once frequented cinemas to watch Marlene

Dietrich's films, before the actress became a public enemy in Nazi Germany. Learning that India had its own film industry amused and intrigued her. The seventh art had travelled far, and now it beckoned her into a new world.

For Hilda, the journey to India symbolised a fresh start. Yet, her heart carried the weight of an eternal fugitive.

"Darling," Fraser interrupted her thoughts, "life is too short, especially in wartime. We never know what's coming next."

"I worry," she confessed. "If the Nazis win, what will become of me as a Jew? And if the Allies win, what will happen to me as a German?" Her words were tinged with despair.

"You'll be safe in the Far East," he reassured her, though his words failed to soothe her entirely.

"You know," she countered, "many countries under British control favour Nazi dominance in hopes of gaining their promised independence." Her insight caught him off guard, revealing her to be not only observant but deeply attuned to global affairs.

Fraser took her hands in his. "Let's get married. That will guarantee your protection."

Her mind raced. A union with a white, Northern European, non-Jewish man symbolised security and stability—a sharp contrast to her precarious existence. Fraser embodied power, but was his proposal rooted in convenience or love?

"But how could we make it work?" she asked, stepping closer to him. "You're a ship's captain, always at sea, and I'm a wanderer with no destination."

"We can make Bombay our base," he suggested. "I'll try to work on routes from Iraq, Aden, or even the UK, so I can see you regularly." Leaning in, he planted a kiss on her powdered cheek.

"So, I'd be a sailor's wife?" she replied with a touch of sarcasm.

"I'll secure a decent life for you in Bombay," he promised.

Turning toward the endless horizon of the Indian Ocean, Hilda pondered the Eastern saying, *kesmat*—God's will. Marrying Captain Fraser seemed far preferable to the prospect of an arranged marriage. But did he truly love her? And more unsettling, did she love him?

As the port drew nearer, her thoughts drifted to her new life in this unfamiliar land. Her existence had begun to mirror the tales of Sinbad from *The Arabian Nights*, a journey into the unknown, filled with wonder and uncertainty.

Chapter Thirty-Three

New Life

Hilda woke to the sound of a rooster crowing from a nearby courtyard. A gentle knock on the door roused her further.

"Come in," she said, with her German-accented English.

The door opened to reveal a local Indian maid, Sunita, dressed in a traditional sari. She carried a tray with a teacup and teapot, walking gracefully toward the mahogany king-sized bed adorned with carved arches and faintly scented with sandalwood from the adjacent drawers. The furniture, clearly new, spoke of a fresh start.

Sunita approached cautiously, avoiding direct eye contact as custom dictated. She poured the steaming, milky tea infused with cardamom and other Indian spices. Hilda, who had grown fond of the rich, fragrant tea, found herself craving it more than her beloved coffee.

Sitting upright, she allowed Sunita to adjust the pillows behind her back. With the first sip, a smile spread across Hilda's face, her mood momentarily lifted.

"Have we received any letters from abroad?" she asked eagerly.

"No, ma'am. Abdul, the porter, checked the post office, but there's no sign of any letters," Sunita replied politely.

The smile faded from Hilda's face, replaced by a frown and lines of worry. She had been anxiously awaiting news from her newlywed husband, with whom she had spent only a brief honeymoon before he was called back to duty. His obligations to the war effort had taken him away, leaving her alone in a foreign land. For the first time in her life, she had experienced a fleeting taste of happiness—only to have it taken away almost immediately.

Her husband had rented a modest house in Bombay's Byculla district near Victoria Gardens, a far cry from her previous struggles as a fugitive. The lifestyle, luxurious by her old standards, had come easily to her. She had embraced the comfort, though she still carried a quiet compassion, often pausing to inquire about the needs of the homeless. Yet, over time, a certain desensitisation crept in, softening her empathy.

"Now I understand the colonial mentality," she confessed to Samha over afternoon tea one day. "And sadly, I find myself behaving the same way."

Hilda had seen less of the Sassoons since arriving in Bombay. Heskeal Sassoon had secured funding to expand his business in India, providing his family with a comfortable lifestyle. Their new home was not far from Hilda's, but their relationship had subtly shifted.

Since Hilda became Mrs. Fraser, she held the upper hand, becoming the centre of attention and a figure of influence, possibly even power. Her Jewish heritage and affiliations were no longer a concern for the British expatriate community, as her husband's prominent position in colonial society shielded her from scrutiny. The Sassoons, now acutely aware of her elevated status, desperately sought her influence—though it was her husband's connections they needed most to secure their own safety and standing.

On the other hand, Hilda felt excluded by some members of the British community in Bombay due to her Germanic roots. To many, being German was synonymous with being the enemy. Few understood that she was a fugitive Jew, while others harboured suspicions that she might be a German spy. Nevertheless, her Aryan appearance and European heritage placed her higher in the social hierarchy of a distinctly segregated society—a structure that Hitler himself regarded as a model for dividing society based on racial rankings. Her days were spent shopping at boutiques catering to Westerners, walking in Victoria Gardens when the weather allowed, or enjoying tea in English salons.

One humid afternoon, Hilda took her usual walk in the gardens, her conservative long-sleeved dress clinging to her in the oppressive heat. As she decided to return home, she noticed footsteps behind her. A jolt of fear coursed through her—muggings had become more frequent with the decline of law and order since the war began, and anti-British sentiment was on the rise.

Before she could react, a strong hand grabbed her arm. She struggled against the grip, her shouts stifled as a large hand covered her mouth. The attacker dragged her beneath a mango tree, its ripe fruit filling the air with sweetness. But an overpowering scent of cologne quickly replaced the fruity aroma.

"Please, don't shout—it's me!"

She turned, recognising the familiar face. "Albert?" she exclaimed in disbelief, her voice sharp with anger as she saw the sweat dripping from his forehead.

"What on earth are you doing here?" she demanded.

"I wanted to surprise you. I was joking," he said sheepishly.

"Stalking me isn't a joke! Forcing me to submit to your whims certainly isn't either!" Her Germanic seriousness was unyielding, her shock evident.

"I miss you, darling. You've been ignoring me," Albert pleaded, his tone desperate.

"You have to understand—I'm married now. I'm loyal to my husband. You're young, with the whole world ahead of you. Besides, your family would never accept this relationship."

"But we love each other!" Albert insisted, nearly dropping to his knees. "We could have married—we're both Jews. That's what matters to my family."

"It's more complicated than you think. We're trying to survive," she said firmly. "This isn't pre-war Baghdad. Those times are gone—wake up, young man."

"But I love you, Hilda," he whispered.

Her voice softened but the tone of conviction was firm. "We don't have the right to love," she said.

Without waiting for his reply, she turned and walked away, her steps echoing on the brick pathway.

As the monsoon rains began to fall, first as light droplets and then in a heavy downpour, Hilda ran, her dress clinging to her as tears streamed down her face. She prayed the rain would wash away her pain, but the ache in her heart remained.

Chapter Thirty-Four

Bad News Travels Fast

Days and months seemed to slip by in a blur. Hilda had gradually accustomed herself to the life of luxury in her newly adopted country, yet a persistent longing for her native Germany — and, at times, Baghdad — tugged at her heart. The war news, often delayed and sporadic, reached them long after the major battles in Europe or the Far East had taken place. The Germans seemed to be gaining the upper hand, though British propaganda deliberately obscured much of the truth to maintain morale and control. Hilda couldn't help but wonder what losing the war would mean for Britain, especially in its colonies, where the call for independence grew louder.

Caught between allegiances to her native Germany and the host countries she had passed through, Hilda felt deeply torn. Stateless, she often felt both accepted and rejected by those around her. Her temporary British residency and travel documents, secured through her marriage to Captain Fraser, provided a sense of stability. But the future remained uncertain, especially as her husband held out hope for a prominent position with a commercial shipping company in Bombay after the war.

Hilda called out to her maid, Sunita, asking if the porter Abdul had gone to the post office. She clung to the hope of receiving a letter from her husband, though months had passed since his last correspondence. His letters described work aboard ships navigating the perilous routes between England and the United States. The mere thought of the dangers he faced terrified her, and she dreaded the local newspapers — *The Bombay Gazette* and *News of India* — which frequently reported on ships assaulted by German torpedoes in the Atlantic.

Her visits to the Sassoons had grown infrequent. Hilda wanted to make it clear to Albert that his advances were unwelcome. This estrangement, coupled with the isolation of being a foreigner, weighed heavily on her. Yet nothing compared to the agony of not knowing her husband's fate.

Sitting alone with her tea at the Irani Café, Hilda tried to focus on the newspaper in front of her. The headline about British ships sunk by German torpedoes brought fresh tears to her eyes. She looked up at the café's high ceiling, its elegant arches and colonial design a reminder of Bombay's complex history. Built by an Iranian Zoroastrian immigrant in the late 19th century, the café had become a refuge for many, including Europeans seeking familiarity in a foreign land.

A waiter approached her table, his usual polite smile tinged with hesitation. Unlike many other Western patrons who treated him with minimal respect, Hilda often acknowledged him with warmth.

"Are you okay, ma'am?" he asked tentatively, fearful of overstepping boundaries with a white woman.

Hilda's despair was evident in her reply. "Who is okay in times like these? It's the war," she said, her voice heavy with sorrow. Sensing her anguish, the waiter respectfully stepped aside.

After paying her bill, the café owner kindly hailed a taxi to escort her home. The porter held the door open as she exited, standing upright with practised precision. The waiter, still shaken, worried that his words might have offended a valued customer, especially one of her stature. Hilda acknowledged the gesture with a faint, apologetic smile but waved off the taxi.

The driver's expression betrayed his disappointment at losing a fare, his livelihood tied to such opportunities. Unfazed, Hilda began walking aimlessly through the streets of Bombay. Her body moved on autopilot, carrying her toward her residence, but her mind was consumed by tormenting images: sinking ships, the cries of wounded sailors, and the vivid, intrusive image of her husband.

These horrors had haunted her since she'd watched the British war film *Convoy* with Samha at Capitol Cinema a few days prior. The stark depiction of naval warfare had only intensified her fears. As she wandered, she tilted her head toward the sky and cried out, her voice breaking the stillness around her.

"Please, God, not another loss."

Chapter Thirty-Five

Life Must Go On

Hilda received some devastating news about her husband. Her intuition had warned her long before the events unfolded. A telegram of condolence had arrived, marking the beginning of a new chapter in Hilda's life. She was summoned by the British governor in Bombay to attend a low-profile ceremony commemorating the war heroes.

Samha had grown increasingly involved in Hilda's personal affairs since her marriage to Captain Fraser, and even more so after hearing the tragic news. The Sassoons re-entered her world, their wealth and status making them a respected part of both British and Indian high society. Hilda's association with the Sassoons elevated her standing in the expatriate community, and Samha, feeling more secure in her own marriage due to her husband's health-related limitations, seemed less concerned about any potential rivalry. Albert, meanwhile, channelled his unfulfilled desires elsewhere, finding solace among Iraqi Jewish women and the occasional visit to Bombay's brothels. Hilda was detached from these dramas, uninterested in participating in Albert's pursuits.

When the day of the commemoration ceremony arrived, Samha accompanied Hilda to show her support — and, perhaps, to gain proximity to the upper echelons of British society. The ceremony concluded with a high tea in a grand hall at the Taj Mahal Palace Hotel. The crowd was more interested in chatting with Hilda, while Samha attempted to mingle with the upper-class British society, aware that they might look down on her as lower class by English standards or even a lower caste in India.

Dignitaries gave speeches praising the bravery of those who had lost their lives in the war. Hilda exchanged a disapproving glance with Samha. They didn't speak, but the unspoken question lingered in both their minds: *They lost their lives... but for what?*

As servants began clearing tables, the crowd began to drift toward the luxurious foyer, its grand design inspired by the palaces of Indian Maharajas. Built in 1903, the Taj Mahal Palace Hotel had become a symbol of colonial grandeur, catering to British, European, and elite Indian clientele. The hotel was named after the Taj Mahal mausoleum in Agra, northern India. This magnificent shrine was built by the Mughal emperor in memory of his beloved wife, who died during childbirth. It remains one of history's most enduring love stories. As Samha recounted the tale behind the hotel's name, Hilda whispered softly, "Will love last forever?"

But Samha failed to grasp the deeper meaning behind Hilda's words. To Samha, Hilda's marriage had always seemed one of convenience rather than love, providing security in an uncertain world, as well as a generous war pension and other benefits from the British government.

Unable to resist, Samha, emboldened by a few shots of whiskey from the ceremony, asked hesitantly, "Did you love Captain Fraser?"

The question hit Hilda like a brick. She turned sharply, her eyes blazing. "Love? What is love? Do you love your husband?"

Samha paused, careful not to offend her friend. "Well," she began slowly, "where I come from, we marry for convenience. Love has little to do with it. Our families arrange everything."

Hilda sighed, her anger softening. "I suppose I'm in a similar position. He was kind, but I hardly knew him. We had a few weeks of happiness — like a dream. For the first time in my life I felt secure, and perhaps it will be the last."

Relieved not to have offended her friend, Samha exhaled deeply.

"I never expected to see such a lavish place. There's nothing like it in Berlin," Hilda said, attempting to change the subject.

"My husband once told me it was built by a local tycoon after he was denied entry to a British hotel — despite his wealth — simply because he wasn't white," Samha replied lifting her head high with pride, eager to demonstrate that her general knowledge was far from modest and that she was just as capable, if not superior, to a Western woman.

Hilda shook her head. "Strange how we treat our fellow humans," she said thoughtfully. Then, with a spark of mischief in her tone, she added, "I fancy a drink. Will you join me?"

Samha looked startled but intrigued. She was the only non-European woman present, apart from a handful of wealthy locals. "If you insist. But don't tell my husband," she whispered.

Hilda giggled, and they found a table. An Indian waiter approached them with a polite bow. "What can I get you ladies?"

"Two whiskeys, please," Hilda replied confidently.

The boldness of her behaviour shocked Samha, who rarely drank alcohol in public without her husband's permission. But Hilda's confidence was contagious. They exchanged smirks, a sense of triumph lighting their faces.

The waiter returned with their drinks, puzzled by the sight of two women from different ethnic backgrounds sitting together. He hesitated, clearly unsure how to categorise them.

Noticing a young white man staring at their table, Hilda raised her voice playfully. "We're both Jewish," she declared, breaking the tension.

Samha stifled a laugh, the man quickly averting his gaze. Their giggles grew louder, attracting disapproving looks from the other patrons. It was unheard of for women — especially in a place like this — to laugh so freely and drink openly.

"Today wine, tomorrow... who knows?" Samha recited in Arabic, quoting the pre-medieval Baghdadi poet Abu Nuwas.

"What does that mean?" Hilda asked.

Samha explained, recounting how the poet had been criticised for drinking alcohol, defying Islamic teachings.

Their laughter echoed through the grand hall, undeterred by the judgmental stares of those around them. For a brief moment, they let go of the burdens of their pasts and the uncertainties of their futures, finding solace in each other's company and the fleeting joy of shared rebellion.

Chapter Thirty-Six

Echoes of the Past

The weather grew increasingly intense as the monsoon season approached, bringing relentless rain and suffocating humidity. Hilda had worked to solidify her connections within the local expat community, hoping to have support in emergencies. However, she remained closer to her Iraqi friends, who offered her much-needed moral support. Samha, ever insistent, managed to draw Hilda out of her isolation and introduce her to members of the Iraqi Jewish society in Bombay. Many of them had fled their homeland, especially after the *Farhud*.

"We're all in the same boat," Samha would say, offering comfort to her grieving friend.

Sunita, Hilda's middle-aged Indian maid, whose facial lines indicated a life of toil, entered the room carrying a tray with steaming coffee and a bowl of creamy rice porridge. The dish, spiced with cinnamon and other aromatic flavours, had become one of Hilda's favourite indulgences. Along with the tray, Sunita also brought a pile of letters, setting them carefully on the table.

Hilda picked up the butter knife to open the letters but quickly abandoned it, her eagerness overtaking her patience. Most of the envelopes contained letters of sympathy from locals, many of whose names she did not recognise. But one particular envelope caught her eye—it bore a stamp with the emblem of the Iraqi monarchy. She tore it open and immediately recognised the handwriting. It was a letter from Nyla and Amin.

She felt immense gratitude to the couple who had saved her life and knew she would remain indebted to them for as long as she lived. Hilda often spoke of Nyla and Amin to her friends in Bombay, saying, "I wouldn't be here if it weren't for them."

The scent of *Dhn al-Ood* perfume wafted from the paper, stirring memories of Iraq. Hilda eagerly read Nyla's words:

Dear Hilda,

I hope this letter finds you well. We miss you dearly. Life here is challenging, but we are managing. Harb has started walking and talking, and I've made sure he knows how to say "Aunty Hilda" properly—well, almost!

The situation in Iraq remains dire. The aftermath of the war and ongoing hardships weigh on everyone, but we endure. We were overjoyed to hear of your marriage. Amin and I wish you all the happiness in the world.

You asked about Kurchia and her family. They went into hiding after the *Farhud*, but I've heard they've since left the country. Many of our Jewish friends are also in hiding or have fled to other countries, some aided by organisations helping them reach Palestine. Despite everything, there's hope. Many friends are starting to reappear, and life is slowly regaining a semblance of normalcy.

Please write back if you need anything.

With love, Nyla and Amin

Attached was an additional note in carefully written German, penned by Amin, reiterating Nyla's message.

Hilda felt overwhelmed by the couple's kindness and the bittersweet memories they stirred. As she sat reflecting, Sunita timidly entered the room. "Ma'am, is the coffee to your liking?" she asked nervously, eager to please her employer.

"It's lovely, thank you," Hilda replied absently, her thoughts still with Nyla and Amin.

Feeling a renewed sense of purpose, Hilda moved to her writing desk, pulled out a notepad, and began drafting a reply. She wrote about her gratitude for their letter, her grief over her husband's loss, and her hope that they might reunite after the war. She also mentioned the Sassoons and their ongoing support.

The phone rang, interrupting her writing.

"Good morning, Hilda. It's Samha," came the familiar voice on the line.

"Of course it is," Hilda responded, attempting a playful tone.

"Do you have time today?"

"Yes, I'm free. I actually wanted to talk to you about our friends in Iraq."

"Are they all right?" Samha's voice was tinged with concern.

"They're fine, not to worry. Where shall we meet?"

"I've discovered a distant cousin who fled to Bombay with his family. His young daughter has become an actress in the Indian film industry."

Hilda raised an eyebrow at the revelation. "Actress? In a film studio? Isn't that something from Berlin or Hollywood?"

"Yes, Bombay has a thriving film industry," Samha explained patiently. "Several Iraqi Jewish girls are acting here, including my niece Rachael. Albert seems quite taken with her, and they might marry."

The mention of Albert struck a nerve. Though Albert had ceased pursuing Hilda after her marriage, his lingering glances had grown more daring since her husband's death. Hilda was relieved to be free, yet deep down, she couldn't deny a lingering yearning for the physical connection she once felt with Albert. Lost in her daydream of a fleeting reunion, Hilda was jolted back to reality by the sharp, high-pitched tone of Samha's voice.

"I'm not sure about that match," Samha continued, her tone dropping. "I've heard rumours about the roles some of these girls take—scenes involving kissing or revealing costumes that the local actresses refuse."

"Come on, it's just Western fashion," Hilda said dismissively. "Have you seen *The Blue Angel* with Marlene Dietrich?"

"Yes, it was a hit back in Baghdad! We watched it at the Al-Zawra Cinema on Al-Rashid Street," Samha said, pride evident in her voice.

"Oh, I remember seeing a few films there with Amin and Nyla," Hilda reminisced. "Nyla adored Rita Hayworth."

Samha smiled but quickly shifted back to her point. "You'll love Regal Cinema here in Bombay. It's grand and elegant."

Sensing the competitive undertone, Hilda decided to redirect the conversation. "I'd like to visit a film set and see how the industry works. It would be interesting to meet your niece."

Both women understood the subtext. Neither truly cared about Rachael's acting career. For Hilda, it was about confronting her unresolved feelings toward Albert. For Samha, it was about asserting her boundaries and testing Hilda's intentions.

"I've also received a letter from Nyla and Amin," Hilda said, changing the subject.

"How are they? They're such a lovely couple, aren't they?"

"Indeed, they are."

"I've become increasingly worried about the Iraqis," Samha admitted, her distress evident.

"The ones who caused the havoc in the Jewish quarter are a minority, indoctrinated by Nazi propaganda," Hilda replied, her tone measured. "I've endured the same on a much larger scale in Germany."

"Let's leave the past behind," Samha said briskly. "Albert will pick you up tomorrow after lunch to visit the studio."

As the call ended, Hilda gazed out at the rain-drenched park. The conversation had stirred something deep within her—a conflict between her desire for love and the guilt of betraying her friend. She whispered to herself, "But I'm alive, and that's what matters."

Chapter Thirty-Seven

The Reunion

Hilda woke earlier than usual, brimming with energy. Was it the golden rays of sunlight streaming through the spotless window, or the anticipation of a new adventure? She couldn't quite tell. The maid hurried to prepare breakfast, while Hilda decided to devote the morning to a long, luxurious bath.

The brass tub was filled with warm water infused with fragrant Indian herbs and dried flowers, ingredients the maid had procured from the old city market. Hilda had insisted on rejuvenating her appearance, requesting the finest herbal blends, even though she'd dismissed such remedies before. Her sudden focus on beauty surprised the maid, who had assumed her mistress would adhere to traditional mourning customs. Among some Indian women, mourning was so sacred that they even embraced the Sati tradition, sacrificing themselves after their husbands' deaths. Yet here was Hilda, shedding her grief for something she refused to admit was vanity.

Standing by the dented brass tub, Hilda caught sight of herself in the silver mirror and let out a soft gasp. "Oh dear," she murmured, confronting the sagging lines of her body. Her maid, alarmed, rushed in to find Hilda in tears.

"Are you alright, ma'am?"

Hilda couldn't answer, but her maid's intuition filled the silence. "You are very pretty, madam," she said soothingly. Though the words comforted Hilda, they couldn't overcome her self-criticism. Dismissing the maid politely, she scrubbed her fair skin with a loofah, dried off, and hurried to her bedroom.

The sight of her late husband's gift—a makeup box—triggered memories of her time in Berlin, where she'd earned money helping wealthy ladies with their cosmetics. Despite this, she felt amateurish applying makeup to herself. The maid, observing discreetly, masked her astonishment. Weren't all Western women skilled in such arts? Apparently not, she mused, watching Hilda struggle.

Hilda spritzed herself with Chantilly perfume, a rare luxury amidst wartime shortages. She recalled the kind British consulate wife in Bombay who had sympathised with her situation, confessing that her own family, like the British royal family, had Germanic roots they couldn't acknowledge.

The maid interrupted her reverie. "Your friends are outside."

"Let them in," Hilda responded, to the maid's surprise.

"I already have, but madam and sir are in a hurry. They want to reach the studio before the film call."

Disappointment flickered in Hilda's eyes. She'd been expecting to see Albert, as his mother had planned. "Is he coming or not?" she wondered silently, casting a critical glance at her reflection and regretting the effort she'd spent preparing.

Outside, she rushed to the waiting Austin car. Albert and Samha sat in the back seat. Albert stepped out, greeting Hilda warmly but cautiously, under his mother's hawk-like gaze. Hilda avoided direct eye contact, feigning nonchalance but failing to fool Samha.

Albert's tailored silk suit complemented his athletic frame, while Samha wore a flowery dress and a white Panama hat. Albert offered his seat to Hilda beside his mother and moved to sit next to the chauffeur.

The car navigated the city's old roads, which soon gave way to bumpy, muddy paths. A wooden sign directed them to Malad, where the vibration from the uneven road jarred Hilda's body. Relief came as they reached the gates of Bombay Talkies studios.

Albert's excitement was palpable as he began explaining the cinema world and how Iraqi Jewish women had found roles in films. Hilda noticed Samha's quiet disapproval—her son's fascination with Hilda was one thing, but the idea of him marrying an actress was entirely unacceptable.

"They take roles that local Indian girls refuse," Samha muttered with disdain, "like indecent scenes."

Hilda pitied Albert, caught between his mother's expectations and his ambitions. She also felt a pang of envy toward Rachel, a rising starlet who embodied youth and beauty.

At the studio, they were warmly received. The manager, eager to impress, offered them rare whiskey and extended a deferential welcome, intrigued by rumours of the Sassoons' potential investments.

Rachel soon arrived, wearing a short skirt and a vest that revealed her midriff and cleavage. In her early twenties, she was stunning, with a confidence that unnerved Hilda. Albert greeted her with a kiss on the cheek, while Samha offered a distant air kiss. Rachel turned to Hilda, saying, "It's nice to meet you," with a curtsy that made Hilda glance around, unsure if the greeting was directed at her. Realising she was the only white person in the room, Hilda mumbled, "Likewise," her voice faint.

As Rachel chatted with Albert, Hilda and Samha feigned interest, focusing instead on the young actress's looks. For different reasons, neither woman approved of Rachel.

"Do you speak English, my dear?" Samha asked pointedly, her tone dripping with condescension.

Rachel's confidence faltered, though she quickly recovered. "Of course," she replied, parroting phrases she'd learned in English school.

An Indian man in a half-sleeved shirt entered, addressing Rachel. "Ma'am, we're ready for you on set."

Rachel stood up proudly. Albert encouraged her with, "Good luck, darling," as she left.

Turning to Hilda, Samha whispered, "Isn't she beautiful?"

"Indeed, she is," Hilda replied, masking her jealousy and anger with difficulty.

"They make a lovely couple," Samha added, gauging Hilda's reaction.

Hilda forced a stoic expression. "They do," she said in a clipped tone, despite her trembling voice betraying her emotions.

Albert broke the tension, brimming with excitement. "Let's go and watch Rachel during the shoot!"

The two women rose, their responses muted and synchronised: "Okay."

Chapter Thirty-Eight

Uncertainty in Wartime

News from the warfront reached British colonies like Bombay at a frustratingly slow pace. Telegraph cables, vulnerable to German sabotage, and propaganda-laden BBC broadcasts offered limited clarity. Yet bad news, as always, travelled fast. The British expatriate community in Bombay was on edge, their fears magnified by the swift Japanese invasion of British territories in the Far East, including Hong Kong and Singapore. Rumours swirled of an impending Axis victory, heightening anxieties.

For Hilda, her identity as a Jewish-German woman was a constant source of unease. The dual threat of persecution—because of her heritage and her religion—strained her already tenuous relationship with the Sassoons. Although Samha and Hilda maintained occasional contact through short visits and sporadic phone calls, their interactions had grown careful, guarded.

One late, humid night at the end of the monsoon season, Hilda lay in bed, absorbed in a German novel she'd found at a second hand bookstall in central Bombay. The familiarity of her native tongue brought her comfort, allowing her to momentarily escape the looming fears of a Japanese invasion that preoccupied the expatriate community.

The sudden, heavy knock at the door shattered her calm. Heart pounding, Hilda froze, debating whether to stay silent or investigate. The knocks grew louder, more insistent, as if delivered by an angry hand. She wanted to pray but found herself unable to recall any words of faith. A bitter thought crept in: if God truly existed, why would He allow such suffering?

Crawling on her knees to the door, she strained to hear a voice. A familiar whisper broke through the noise. "Hilda, it's me."

Even as the words registered, anxiety clouded her mind. "Who are you?" she demanded, her voice unsteady.

A pause hung in the air, deepening her unease. Then, in Arabic: "I'm Samha. Please, open the door."

Relief washed over Hilda as recognition finally broke through her fear. Adrenaline surged as she stood, unbolted the door, and found herself face-to-face with her friend. But the sight of Samha was startling—her usually polished appearance with full make-up was replaced by dishevelled clothes, her face streaked with smudged kohl.

"Are you and your family okay?" Hilda asked, her voice trembling.

"I don't know," Samha replied, her tone frantic. "I don't know!"

Hilda, accustomed to the heightened emotional responses of her friend's culture, recognised this was more than typical hysteria. Her next question slipped out involuntarily. "Is Albert okay?"

Samha's agitation paused, and she turned to Hilda with an accusing glare. "Is that all you care about?"

Hilda flushed with embarrassment. "No, I meant... the boys," she stammered, attempting to recover.

"You're right to ask," Samha conceded, her voice heavy with anguish. "He is the problem. Albert has decided to volunteer for the British army. He heard about the Japanese advances—the fall of Hong Kong—and now he's determined to fight."

Samha broke into sobs, collapsing into Hilda's embrace. Tears streamed down her face, leaving black trails of kohl on Hilda's skin.

"I know what you mean," Hilda said softly, though her words lacked comfort. "I've been listening to German broadcasts. There's pressure on the Japanese to persecute all Europeans—including Jews."

Samha nodded, her voice cracking. "It's the same hatred that's pushed Albert to take such a drastic step. I don't know what I'll do if I lose him." She buried her face in Hilda's chest, her grief spilling out.

Hilda's thoughts drifted, unbidden, to her own son. Still so young when they'd been separated. Was he alive? Dead? Free? Imprisoned? Her mind wandered further, imagining details she didn't want to consider—had he experienced love? Was he alone? The weight of these questions brought fresh tears to her eyes.

Hilda blinked them away, her practical nature asserting itself. "What are you going to do?" she asked, her voice steadying.

Samha hesitated. "My husband wants to send us to South Africa. He says his business partners can arrange safe passage. But..." Her voice broke again. "I can't leave Albert behind. I just can't."

Hilda felt a pang of pity. She knew all too well the agony of separation, the shame of leaving someone behind to an uncertain fate. "Don't worry," she said gently, squeezing Samha's hand. "I'm here for you."

The two women embraced tightly, sharing their grief and fears in silence. Outside, the humid night pressed in, heavy with the weight of the unknown.

Chapter Thirty-Nine

Parting Shadows

The streets of Bombay appeared sombre, despite the bright sun and the milder temperatures that followed the monsoon. The roads were quieter than before; white faces had grown scarce, appearing only briefly as they hurried to cars or entered government and financial institutions. Anti-British sentiment was mounting. The Indian nationalist movement had gained momentum, bolstered by the Allies' losses in Europe and the Far East. The Japanese, promising independence after an Axis victory, fuelled the resistance against British rule.

Hilda, caught in this charged atmosphere, confined herself to her home. With her British identification—a result of her marriage to a British citizen—she was seen as a colonial subject, a position fraught with danger. Initially, she thought the document might solve her problems, but it soon became a liability. Stripped of her German nationality by Nazi decree. Regardless, her Northern European appearance made her stand out easily among the angry crowds targeting British or European residents in Bombay. Hilda wondered if the locals' behaviour toward Europeans had shifted, including her maid who seemed less deferential, taking frequent, unauthorised leaves. Hilda often wondered whether this was paranoia or her new reality.

Her days passed in uneasy isolation. She read books and newspapers, listened to the radio, and occasionally prepared her own meals when her maid was absent. Venturing out had become a risk, so she relied on the maid or the porter for groceries.

One evening, she sat in her armchair, a glass of Lion beer in hand, its quality still the subject of her internal debate compared to German brews. The German radio station droned on, exalting Nazi victories, only deepening her despondency. Suddenly, a loud banging at the door jolted her.

Heart racing, she stood and switched off the radio, straining her ears. Could it be the Japanese? Nazi propaganda had claimed their forces were days away from taking Bombay, stirring fears among the city's European residents. She decided to remain quiet, extinguishing the lights. But the knocking grew louder, more insistent, until she could no longer ignore it.

Creeping toward the door, she whispered shakily, "Who is it?"

"It's me, Hilda. Open the door," a familiar voice responded.

Relief and dread intermingled as she recognised the voice. Without hesitation, she unlatched the door, and the handle was pushed from the outside with urgency. There stood Albert, his face intense with emotion.

"Darling!" she exclaimed.

He entered quickly, closing the door behind him. Before she could say another word, he pulled her into a tight embrace and began kissing her feverishly. Overwhelmed, she returned his kisses, her hands exploring the contours of his body. In the dim light, she noticed his British Army uniform, which only heightened her desire.

"I missed you," he said breathlessly between kisses.

"Me too, darling," she murmured.

Before she could say more, Albert swept her into his arms and carried her to the bedroom. Resistance seemed futile, and she surrendered herself to the moment, her fears and loneliness melting away under the weight of his passion.

Later, as they lay tangled in the sheets, she broke the silence. "What's going to happen to you?"

"I don't know," he admitted. "I've been conscripted into the British Army and posted to the Far East—perhaps Burma."

A tear slipped down her cheek. "I'm worried about you."

He sighed. "I have no choice. My family is still in limbo, unsure whether to return to Iraq now that the British have regained control, or to relocate to South Africa, far from Nazi influence. Either way, I'm a target—under the Germans or the Japanese. And they've promised me British citizenship after the war."

"And your fiancée?" Hilda's voice carried an edge of envy.

"You mean Rachel?" Albert said, shaking his head. "She's focused on becoming a movie star in India. The arranged marriage isn't working, and my mother wouldn't approve of such a union anyway. Female actors don't garner much respect in our society."

A selfish thought surged within Hilda: *If I can't have him, no one will.* She leaned in to kiss him again, her lips demanding and desperate. Albert responded, pulling her close, the creaking of the old wooden bed filling the room like a lullaby of transient comfort.

Chapter Forty

A Fragile Sense of Home

The atmosphere in Bombay grew more solemn with each passing day. News of Allied failures in the war dominated the headlines. The Imperial Japanese Army had conquered the majority of British, French, and Dutch colonies in the Far East. Their discipline and unwavering ideology made neighbouring Southeast Asian nations fearful of being next on Japan's expansionist agenda.

Meanwhile, the Nazis advanced triumphantly through Europe and North Africa. For expatriates in British-controlled India, news from Europe became overshadowed by the escalating tensions in Asia. The anti-Western sentiment among the Indian population had reached boiling point.

"If they cannot defend themselves, how can they defend others?" Sunita, Hilda's maid, remarked one day, her voice carrying an uncharacteristic boldness that left Hilda stunned. The change in Sunita's attitude was abrupt, yet it reflected the growing discontent among Indians, fed up with British exploitation. Confidence in the idea of self-rule had been building as British forces dwindled in India, leaving the colonial authorities struggling to maintain control. With the British relying heavily on Indian soldiers to fight in Europe, Japanese espionage flourished in Bombay, fuelling the nationalist movement.

Communication between London and its colonies had weakened, further diminishing the British presence. The independence movement, however, largely overlooked the implications of Nazi ideology. Ironically, Hitler admired the British colonial system in India, aspiring to model a hierarchical society on its rigid caste and class structures.

Hilda knew her fate was tied to the British Empire. As a British citizen and a Jew, she stood no chance of fitting into Nazi ideology should the Axis powers triumph. Yet, it was still safer to be British than a German Jew.

Her days passed in anxious anticipation of news from Albert. His letters had become infrequent, a consequence of the war's increasing ferocity. She cautiously sought updates from Samha, who was no better off; her family, as Iraqi Jewish refugees, lived under the fragile protection of British power. Albert's deployment to the perilous Far East had only deepened their shared anxiety.

One evening, Hilda picked up the heavy, unwieldy telephone handset and dialled the number she had memorised. A faint, cautious voice answered.

"Hello?"

"Hello, Samha. It's Hilda," she said, pausing to gauge Samha's mood. For a moment, there was silence, as though Samha debated whether to speak or let the call end. Finally, she responded.

"I know who you are. How are you?" Samha's tone was guarded, a reflection of the pervasive fear surrounding them.

"I'm fine. I'd like to see you," Hilda said, trying to sound composed.

"Of course, we'd love to, but..." Samha's hesitation hung in the air.

"I understand," Hilda said, sensing the unspoken concern. "I know a place where we could meet safely. It's neither too public nor entirely private. I'm aware of the risks involved in being seen with someone like me." Her directness, a product of her Germanic upbringing, cut through the tension.

Samha remained silent, shame creeping into her hesitation. Her darker, olive-toned complexion allowed her to blend in, passing as an Indian or a Pathan woman. But Hilda's European features betrayed her origins, making her a glaring target in Bombay's charged atmosphere.

"I just wanted to check on you and your family," Hilda added gently.

Another uncomfortable pause ensued before Hilda finally broached the subject she had been dreading.

"Have you heard anything from Albert?"

There was a sudden commotion on the other end, followed by a man's harsh voice.

"Hello, Hilda."

It took her a moment to recognise Mr. Sassoon. His voice, normally measured and dignified, now carried an edge of fear and sorrow.

"Hello. Is everything okay?" Hilda's voice trembled, laden with worry.

"No. We've had no word from Albert since his posting to Burma. His garrison reportedly surrendered to the Japanese. The news is grim." His voice cracked, breaking into sobs. Hilda listened helplessly to the muffled sounds of a father's grief.

Fighting back her own emotions, she offered, "Do you want me to come over?"

"No, thank you. You have your own troubles. We've decided to return to Iraq," he said, his tone softening with a glimmer of resolve.

"How will you manage that? Isn't it dangerous?"

"We'll travel through Iran by train and car. Many in our community are returning. Iraq has been our people's home for thousands of years, and it will be for thousands more." His voice filled with pride, masking the uncertainty of their plan.

Hilda's thoughts raced. "But the journey is perilous, and sympathy for Jews in Iran is scarce." She realised the precariousness of her situation—British, German, and Jewish. There seemed to be no safe path for her.

"True, but the Anglo-Soviet invasion of Iran has given us hope. The situation may improve," he replied, his words tinged with cautious optimism.

Lowering his voice, he added, "Have you heard of the Zionist movement?"

Caught off guard, Hilda hesitated. "I've heard of it. Isn't it just a group of intellectuals with unrealistic ambitions?"

"Not anymore," he said gravely. "It has become a militant effort to establish a Jewish homeland in Palestine. It might be our only future. Look at us now—scattered and uprooted because of who we are."

Hilda was taken aback by his fervour. "How could such a thing ever be realised?" she asked, half in disbelief.

"I don't know. But perhaps it's the only way forward," he replied, bitterness and hope mingling in his voice.

Samha gently took the phone from her husband, her voice soothing. "I wish we could all return to our original homes."

The word *home* lingered in Hilda's mind. What was home? And where could she ever truly call home again? Her last hope of building a family had vanished, leaving her with the bitter realisation that home was no more than a mirage—something that receded further the closer she tried to reach it.

Chapter Forty-One

Lost Love

The days seemed endlessly long for Hilda, who remained practically confined to her flat in isolation. The maid had taken over much of the daily household management, almost as if she was the mistress of the house. Hilda, mindful not to upset her, remained courteous despite the subtle shifts in power. She had always treated her maids with respect, having worked in wealthy German households herself. Her guiding principle had been to never undermine others, particularly those often dismissed as "little people."

Yet, caution coloured every aspect of her life now. Any correspondence from the British authorities was promptly destroyed for fear that the maid might read it and pass the information to nationalist groups—or worse, to the Japanese authorities if the tide of war turned unfavourably.

Since the Sassoon family had departed, Hilda felt an immense void in her life. Only now did she fully realise how much Samha's companionship had meant to her. Their shared struggles—being far from home and wrestling with uncertainty—had been a balm for her spirit.

One morning, Hilda entered the kitchen where the maid was preparing coffee. The routine had changed; instead of the maid bringing coffee to the living room, Hilda now retrieved it herself. Resigned to this new order, she carried her coffee back to her bedroom and tuned in to her old radio for news. The broadcast was a cacophony of conflicting reports, and Hilda struggled to discern the truth amidst the propaganda.

A faint noise outside drew her attention. Startled, she left her room and walked cautiously to the living room. Her gaze fell on a small brown suitcase by the window. Memories of her life in Germany flooded back—the suitcase had always been ready, a silent symbol of her transient, precarious existence.

"*Must I always live with a suitcase at my side?*" she thought bitterly, her mind wandering back to Bombay as the outside noise subsided.

On the dining table lay a pile of letters, carelessly left by the maid. Anxiously, Hilda sifted through them, searching for any familiar names—Albert's or perhaps Samha's. Her heart raced as she opened an envelope from the British Ministry of Defence. It concerned her widow's pension, acknowledging her as a war widow. The dense legal language required her to consult her Oxford English-German dictionary, but the effort was worth it. The letter reassured her that she would receive a steady income sufficient for a decent, if modest, life in India.

Her thoughts were interrupted by the sound of footsteps. Hastily, she slipped the letter into her dress, hiding it against her chest.

"I must visit my family soon," the maid announced as she entered the room. For once, Hilda didn't object. In fact, she felt a flicker of relief—her home had become suffocating.

"They live in Punjab, and it's a long journey," the maid added curtly, her tone growing bolder.

"Please, feel free to go," Hilda replied, her voice subdued.

"I need some money," the maid demanded bluntly.

Hilda was taken aback. She had already paid the maid two months' wages in advance but decided not to argue. Avoiding eye contact, she murmured, "Of course, I'll get it."

As the maid left the room, Hilda noticed her wearing a pair of Oxford shoes—ones her late husband had gifted her from London. The maid wobbled in the high heels, unaccustomed to them. Hilda's heart sank, but she held her tongue. Slowly, she walked to her oak chest to retrieve the money. When she opened the drawer, her heart clenched—her emerald bracelet was gone.

Though anger bubbled under the surface, she quelled it. Resigned to her circumstances, she took out a bundle of rupees and handed it over, silently hoping she would not see the maid again.

Later, as she reorganised her remaining possessions, her hand lingered on an old letter addressed to her. The name "Albert" was scrawled across the back. Her heart quickened as she opened it. She had read this letter countless times before and could almost recite it from memory.

Her eyes skimmed the familiar words, savouring each line until they reached the final declaration: *"I love you."*

The letter mentioned Albert's training camp somewhere in India and his impending posting to the Far East. Hilda clutched the paper tightly, whispering to herself, *"I love you too."*

Chapter Forty-Two

Shattered Hopes

The days brought a glimmer of optimism as the tides of war began to shift. The active involvement of American forces alongside the Allies on both the eastern and western fronts filled the news with hope. Hilda, for her part, finally found some relief in her solitude after her maid left to visit family in Punjab. Without the maid's constant presence and vindictive behaviour, Hilda felt free to move about her flat without fear of scrutiny.

Hilda had even taken the extraordinary step of offering the maid a final settlement to end her service—a bold, almost unheard-of action in Raj-era India. Yet, despite taking the money, the maid continued to appear sporadically, as though she dictated the terms of her employment.

Meanwhile, the expatriate community began to breathe easier. The announcement of U.S. support for the Allied forces seemed to buoy their spirits, and they returned to cafes and restaurants with a renewed sense of confidence, exuding the pride of victors. However, beneath the surface, the brewing nationalist movement persisted, with murmurs of independence continuing to grow among the local population.

Hilda, embracing her newfound independence, enjoyed preparing her own breakfast and coffee—just as she used to in Germany. One morning, the building's porter, an Indian teenage boy, knocked on her door with a bundle of letters. Letters had become her lifeline, a tenuous connection to the outside world and a source of both comfort and anxiety.

As she tipped the boy, his face lit up with delight, and he ran off with a cheerful shout. Hilda, smiling faintly at his reaction, returned to her table. She poured herself a cup of coffee and eagerly sorted through the letters, her hands trembling slightly. Each envelope was examined not for its address but for the sender's name.

One letter immediately captured her attention—it bore stamps featuring the Iraqi monarchy. She reached for a butter knife and opened the envelope in haste, the greasy wrapper slipping to the floor. Holding her breath, she began to read aloud:

Dear Hilda,

I hope you are well. We all miss you and often think of the good times we shared on our journey. Together, we endured both joy and hardship, creating memories that will last a lifetime.

Let me tell you about our journey from India to Iran. We travelled by train, bus, car, and even mule in some parts. My husband chose to avoid major Iranian cities to steer clear of any lingering anti-Jewish sentiment, given the Shah's sympathies with the German Nazi regime. Thankfully, we encountered kindness along the way. When we reached the Arabic-speaking province of Ahwaz, we crossed the magnificent Shatt al-Arab river in Basra—a sight I will never forget. From there, we boarded a train to Baghdad.

I cannot describe the joy I felt upon arriving home. There is something sacred about being in one's own country, in the house of one's ancestors. I long to live out my days and, when the time comes, die in my own bed.

I've seen Amin and Nyla, and they couldn't stop talking about you. They remain loyal friends.

I also searched for Kurchia but could not find her. I heard she left Iraq after the violence, perhaps settling in Palestine. Many from our Jewish community were enticed to leave with promises of prosperity in the so-called Promised Land, though I'm not sure what to believe.

Hilda, I have some very difficult news to share. I've just learned that Albert is a prisoner of war, captured by the Japanese in Burma. The thought of it breaks my heart. His photograph is soaked with my tears—I cry every night, not knowing his fate.

I know how much he meant to you, and I believe he loved you, too. I must also admit that I may have been an obstacle between you.

For that, I ask your forgiveness. Life is often cruel, and we don't always know how to make things right.

Yours,

Samha

Hilda's hands trembled as she finished the letter. Tears streamed down her face, her sobs growing louder until they filled the room. She clutched the letter to her chest, her voice trembling as she whispered through the tears, *"Is this the end?"*

Chapter Forty-Three

Victory's Shadow

The outcome of the war had finally tipped decisively in favour of the Allies. The United States' entry into the conflict and Hitler's disastrous decision to invade the Soviet Union had marked turning points. Hilda held a copy of the *News of India* in her hands, her eyes scanning the headlines of Allied triumphs. A faint smirk crossed her thin lips, painted in crimson lipstick.

"Hitler's greatest mistake was invading Russia," she said quietly, addressing Glenda, the wife of a British consulate official. They were seated together in the lounge of the Taj Mahal Hotel, sipping coffee. "And worse, turning Stalin into an enemy."

"You must be very happy," Glenda said abruptly, interrupting her own sip of tea as though eager to make the point.

"Happy?" Hilda repeated, puzzled.

"Yes, with the war nearly over, and victory in sight, you might finally return to your native country," Glenda added, her words laced with optimism.

Hilda stared at her friend, her face betraying no emotion, though her mind reeled. Return? The idea struck her like a blow. She hadn't considered it. The question of what her future might hold was one she had deliberately avoided, choosing instead to live moment by moment, day by day.

"I'm not sure," Hilda replied softly, her voice distant. "I don't know where to go—or what's left for me."

She gazed at the ornate ceiling, her thoughts drifting away. Her life had become an endless string of losses. Her son, lost to war in Germany. Her family, scattered or dead in Baghdad. Her love, Albert, likely gone in Burma. She wondered if she should follow her heart and search for her loved ones, scattered across distant places.

India offered comfort and stability, even a certain lifestyle, but it wasn't home. And she missed her loved ones—the family she once had, the son she would never see again, and the man she could never truly call hers. She had tried, in vain, to locate them. The Red Cross office in Bombay had offered no answers, no trace of her son or the remnants of her Jewish family. Most had perished or fled Germany during its darkest days.

Glenda watched Hilda with quiet sympathy. Her own family had fled Germany before the war, seeking refuge in England, and she understood what it meant to feel uprooted, unmoored.

Hilda's thoughts turned to Albert. According to the latest letter from Samha, his family had long since abandoned hope of finding him. Rumours suggested that Albert was among the British and Anglo-Indian forces enslaved by the Japanese to build the Burma-Thailand railway, a brutal project that had claimed countless lives. Survivors were few, and the Red Cross had no news of him.

Deep down, Hilda knew the truth. There was no hope of finding Albert alive in such chaos. Even if he had survived, their connection would have been impossible. He was much younger than her, and neither his family nor the society they lived in would have approved of their bond.

Her love for him remained, but it had become a shadow—a memory she clung to in the absence of anything else. Memories were all she had left now: fragments of her past, faces and voices that lived only in her mind.

"Hilda?" Glenda's voice was soft, but it pulled her back from her reverie. "Are you all right? You seemed so far away."

Hilda smiled faintly, though her eyes glistened with unshed tears. "I was in Berlin... Baghdad... Bombay."

The End